PLANEWALKER
by
ALEC R ZEELIE

Planewalker

Alec R. Zeelie

Published by Alec R. Zeelie, 2021.

This is a work of fiction. Similarities to real people, places, or events are entirely coincidental.

PLANEWALKER

First edition. July 21, 2021.

Copyright © 2021 Alec R. Zeelie.

ISBN: 979-8201188726

Written by Alec R. Zeelie.

Also by Alec R. Zeelie

The Runners Series - Book 1
Beyond the Grid

The Runners series - Book 3
Voids

The Runners series - Book 4
The Betrayer

The Runners series - Book 5
Zodiac Games

The Runners series - Book 6
The Long Road Home

Standalone
Legacy of the Destroyer
Ghost Towns: The Runners series - Book 2
Planewalker

CHAPTER I
1

It was late afternoon in the big city. There was bumper to bumper traffic in the middle of the city and most of the pedestrians on the sidewalks looked like they were all late for appointments. Everyone was in a hurry. That was the norm for people living in the big city. The stock traders, investors, business owners, and successful young entrepreneurs who mostly lived on the north side of the city were all used to the hustle and bustle of everyday life in the big city for anyone who wanted to make it big and who wanted to become rich. Few of them ever traveled past the tracks to the south side of the city.

The south side of the city looked nothing like the rest of the city. There were no big houses, restaurants, or office buildings. There were apartment buildings, small grocery stores, and dirty streets where many street vendors tried to make a living by selling everything from food and clothing to illegal drugs.

On the eighth floor of one of the apartment buildings, Kathy was asleep in her small apartment. For a single twenty-seven year old who worked for one of the richest women in the city, her life for the past three years had consisted of very little other than working and trying to help the poor people in her neighborhood. She was tossing and turning on her bed. She was having a nightmare. In her nightmare, she saw herself running between the trees and bushes in a forest. She saw a man and woman armed with strange-looking short swords chasing after her. Even in her nightmare, she could feel the fear, despair and horror as she saw the man and the woman catching her and savagely killing her. She woke up gasping for air and felt a numbing pain shoot through her entire body. She remained motionless on her bed for a few minutes, during which she felt tingling sensations on every part of her body. Hearing the sound of a couple arguing in one of the apartments across the hall from hers, she took her phone from her bedside table and saw what time it was. Yawning as she got out of bed, she ran her fingers through her long black hair before looking for something warm to wear. Her apartment felt cold inside. After filling the kettle for a cup of coffee, she began looking through her fridge and kitchen cupboards, trying to find something quick and easy to prepare for herself. Judging by the few items of furniture she owned and how empty her apartment looked that she was dirt poor. She wasn't rich, but she was richer than most of the people in her neighborhood. She chose to live like this.

While Kathy was enjoying her cup of coffee and preparing a meal for herself, there was a knock at her door. She quickly ran to her bedroom and did what she always did when there was a knock at the door. There had been so many robberies, rapes and murders in her neighborhood that she made it a habit to have her gun ready every time someone knocked on her door. She took her 9mm semi-automatic pistol out from the small safe under her bed, ran to the door and slowly opened it. She breathed a sigh of relief when she saw it was only Diego, the son of one of her neighbors. She kept the pistol hidden as she greeted the boy. She could tell he was feeling shy and embarrassed by the way he kept looking at the floor as he spoke.

"Sorry to bother you, Miss Kathy. My mamma wants to know if you could maybe help us with some food for dinner," he asked.

Diego's family was but one of many in their apartment building who came to her every now and then for some form of help. She couldn't always give everyone exactly what they wanted but she always found a way to help everyone who came to her. Not having any family, she regarded a few of the families in her building as family. The boy waited out in the hall as she quickly took a grocery bag and filled it with a number of food items from her freezer and kitchen cupboards. She handed the bag to the boy, he thanked her and left. After shutting the door, she finished preparing her dinner and ate. While doing this, she kept looking at the clock on the wall. There was still an hour and twenty minutes left before she had to go to work.

Once she'd finished her dinner and washed the dishes, she began getting dressed for work. The black suit she always wore to work, and the fact that she only worked nights made a few of the people in her building think she was either involved in organized crime or an assassin. She was busy putting on her shiny black boots when her cellphone rang. When she looked at the screen and saw who was phoning her, she sighed and cleared her throat before she answered it.

"Hello Mrs Jane. How may I help you?"

"Kathy, before you come to my office, go pick up my shoes and red outfit at my place. I have plans to go out tonight. Don't be late."

Mrs Jane hung up before Kathy could reply. Kathy finished putting on her boots, put on her coat, put her pistol in its holster, grabbed her helmet and left her apartment.

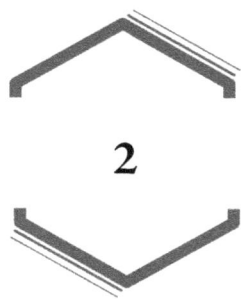

2

Riding on her motorcycle, Kathy was on her way to Mrs Jane's mansion. She knew that whenever Mrs Jane spoke about *'my place'* she was referring to her mansion, and when she spoke about *'my crash nest'* she was referring to her penthouse apartment in the middle of the city. She knew every backstreet and alley she had to take to avoid traffic.

When she arrived at Mrs Jane's mansion, the butler was waiting at the gate along with one of the guards. The butler greeted her and handed her two beautifully designed leather bags with Mrs Jane's outfit and shoes in them. She looked at the large mansion one more time before she left. As she rode away, she wondered for the umpteenth time how someone as mean and heartless as Mrs Jane deserved to live like royalty.

Kathy made her way to Mrs Jane's office building as fast as she could. Taking as many shortcuts as she could, she still knew she was going to be late. With so much traffic in the streets, she only arrived at the office building fifteen minutes after her shift had started. As always, she had to leave her motorcycle between the four other parked cars in the alley behind the building. She and – as Mrs Jane referred to them – *the less important staff*, had to park their vehicles next to the trashcans in the alley. Kathy took off her helmet as she walked to the back entrance door. She used her key card to unlock the door and entered the small search room where she had to take out her pistol and her work ID card. She placed both on the counter and pushed them through the opening underneath the bulletproof glass window, behind which a chubby security guard dressed in a red uniform sat. Kathy and this security guard had seen each other virtually every day since she started working for Mrs Jane. Like most of the people who also worked for her, he never greeted her and never showed any emotions. It was as if everyone who worked there switched off their human side and switched to robot mode at work. The security guard used a small scanner to scan her work ID before he said, "You're on the clock. You're late too."

Kathy put her helmet on the shelf next to the door before she showed him the leather bags and was then asked to show him the contents of the bags. After doing so, he scanned the small bar code on the side of her pistol to make sure it was a firearm issued to her by the company and not an illegal firearm. He gave her work ID and pistol back to her and pressed the green button underneath the counter to open the door to the office building. Kathy put her pistol back in its holster and entered the narrow stairwell. When the door closed behind her, she felt claustrophobic. She began making her way up the stairs to the top floor. This stairwell was just for Mrs Jane's less important employees. All of her other employees used the underground parking area, used the main entrance doors and the elevators to get to their offices.

It took Kathy a full five minutes to make her way up the stairs to the top floor. When she reached the top of the stairs and used her key card to open the door, the angry looking man on the other side of the door said, "Finally. You took your sweet time. Learn to work faster."

He brushed past her and began making his way down the stairs. He was Mrs Jane's day bodyguard. He was only allowed to leave once Kathy arrived for night bodyguard duty. She walked up to the glass doors and entered Mrs Jane's office. The massive office was decorated with modern art and only one painting of Mrs Jane and her husband. In the far left corner was a small desk and computer where Mrs Jane's assistant worked. On the right was a large conference table with chairs all around it, and a large screen on the wall next to it. Mrs Jane's desk looked like it belonged in an art museum. Sitting on the throne-like chair behind her desk, Mrs Jane didn't say a word when Kathy greeted her. She just pointed at the leather bags and snapped her fingers. Kathy began walking towards her desk to give her the bags when Mrs Jane's assistant ran up to her, took the bags from her and gave them to Mrs Jane. The assistant was a pathetic little man. Dressed in a brown suit, the skinny little man didn't have a life. He spent his every waking hour running around, doing things for Mrs Jane. If he wasn't busy working on his computer for her, he was busy doing whatever she told him to do. Mrs Jane took the outfit and shoes out of the bags and looked at them. Her assistant began complementing her taste in clothes and was about to tell her how beautiful she was going to look in that outfit when Mrs Jane got up, pointed at his face and silenced him. The bright yellow outfit she had on was so bright that it almost appeared to glow with the bright lights shining on it.

"You can stop kissing my ass for now, you little worm," Mrs Jane said as she stepped out from behind her desk. "I'm going out tonight, so you better bring your laptop along because I want all four of those reports on my desk in the morning."

She pointed at Kathy and her assistant, snapped her fingers and pointed at the door. Both of them knew that that was their cue to get out of the office. They left the office and stood outside the door with their backs to the door. Mrs Jane got undressed and put on the outfit Kathy had brought. She put on lipstick that matched the color of her outfit and took a small bottle of perfume out of her desk drawer that cost more that Kathy earned in a four months. The strong smell of the perfume made Kathy hold her breath when Mrs Jane opened the door and said, "We're leaving in five minutes. I have a busy night ahead."

She stepped out of her office, slowly walked up to the big mirror on the wall next to the elevator and stared at herself. Kathy and the assistant rushed to the assistant's desk. She used the phone to call

Mrs Jane's chauffeur while the assistant copied a number of work files from his PC onto his laptop. Minutes later, they escorted Mrs Jane into the elevator. Kathy tried to hold her breath as long as she could not to breathe in the smell of the perfume. To her, it smelled like a combination of musk, lavender, gasoline and cat piss. She didn't care how popular or expensive it was, she wouldn't wear it even if she was given to her as a gift.

Outside, the chauffeur stood waiting next to the black limo that was parked in Mrs Jane's private parking area next to the building. Kathy and the assistant escorted Mrs Jane out of the building through a door at the side of the building that nobody else was allowed to use. The chauffeur opened the door for Mrs Jane. Without even looking at him to greet him, she told him to which restaurant she wanted to be taken. Kathy and the assistant got into the limo. As the limo began driving away from the office building, the two had to listen to Mrs Jane as she called one of her lovers on her cellphone.

3

At the restaurant, Kathy stood in a dark corner close to the rest rooms along with four other bodyguards of wealthy business owners who were dining on the best food money could buy. Kathy kept a close eye on Mrs Jane as she enjoyed her dinner and red wine. Half way through her meal, she was joined by a handsome young man. He was one of Mrs Jane's lovers. Although she was married and her husband was just as wealthy as she was, she took advantage of every opportunity she could to feed her hunger for sexual gratification, attention, and a feeling of control. As much as Kathy wanted to inform her husband that Mrs Jane was nothing more than a well dressed classy whore, she knew that she would be fired on the spot.

After dining for more than two hours, Mrs Jane paid for her meal and walked out of the restaurant with her lover by her side. Kathy followed close behind them. They made their way to the limo which was parked in the VIP parking area behind the restaurant. Mrs Jane told her chauffeur and assistant to get out of the limo and go for a walk. Like Kathy, they too knew exactly what that meant. The assistant took his laptop and placed it on top of a trashcan before he continued with his work. Kathy and the chauffeur walked over to an empty parking space close to the restaurant's back entrance. Neither of them spoke a word to each other. They were disgusted by what Mrs Jane was doing and they felt ashamed to work for her. Both of them tried to keep themselves busy by looking at the fancy cars and limos parked in front of them just so that they wouldn't imagine what kinky sexual acts Mrs Jane and her lover were busy performing in the back of the limo.

Fifteen minutes later, Mrs Jane's lover got out of the limo. He tucked his shirt – which was now missing three buttons – into his pants and smiled as he walked away from the limo. He grinned as he walked past Kathy and went back into the restaurant. The assistant took his laptop and joined Kathy and the chauffeur. They knew they had to wait for Mrs Jane to call them before any of them got back into the limo. One of her previous bodyguards had made the mistake a number of years earlier which had cost him his job. After a quick sex session with one of her lovers in the back of the limo, that bodyguard waited for the lover to leave and when he opened the rear door of the limo to get in, he found Mrs Jane still half naked and was fired on the spot.

After about five minutes of waiting in silence, the limo's rear door was opened and Mrs Jane yelled at them, "Come on! We have to get going! The night is still young!"

Kathy and the assistant felt disgusted as they got into the limo. Neither of them could stop themselves from imagining what sexual acts had been performed right where they were sitting. While the assistant continued with his work to take his mind off of what had just happened, Kathy couldn't stop herself from wondering what was wrong with Mrs Jane. She'd known since she started working for her that Mrs Jane was a snobbish and rude woman, and rather heartless with anyone whom she employed, but what she couldn't wrap her head around was why she was such a sex obsessed slut. She'd seen and spoken to Mrs Jane's husband a number of times at the mansion and when he came to the office building. To her, he seemed like a hard working man who used every opportunity he saw to do business or to start a new side business. As busy as he was, she could tell that he kept trying to spoil Mrs Jane with gifts and romantic dinners hoping that it might reignite the flame of love in their marriage. Kathy not only hated Mrs Jane for all her illicit sexual affairs, she also pitied her husband for believing that his wife loved him when it was so obvious that she felt absolutely nothing for him. Kathy wondered if she would ever meet someone special. She wasn't looking for some sugar daddy to give her a better life. Unlike Mrs Jane, Kathy wasn't looking for some handsome hunk who could rock her world in the bedroom every other day, and then leave until their next sexual rendezvous. She was looking for someone with whom she could connect on an emotional level and who also wanted to do something good in the world. Someone who wanted to have a positive impact on people's lives in some way, shape or form. Someone who wasn't only going to be with her through the good times and leave her at the first sign of rough times.

Kathy was trying to paint a picture in her mind of what the perfect man for her would look like when she began feeling a strange tingling sensation in her right hand. She felt slightly dizzy as the sensation spread through her entire hand and began moving up her forearm. She tried to keep an emotionless face and not show any signs of panic as she felt the sensation slowly spread throughout her entire body. She knew that Mrs Jane wouldn't be too happy if she appeared to be sick or appeared to be feeling weak for whatever reason. Luckily for her, Mrs Jane didn't notice anything. She was too busy giving her assistant an insulting speech about how, even if he worked twice as hard and put in double the number of working hours, he would still never be as successful and as rich as any of her *'male friends'* (lovers). Kathy breathed a quiet sigh of relief when the sensation slowly faded away. After Mrs Jane finished her insult session with her assistant, she phone another one of her lovers and asked if he had any plans for the rest of the night. Kathy and the assistant looked at each other and quietly sighed when they heard Mrs Jane tell her lover to meet her at a popular nightclub. They'd both escorted her to that nightclub before with her other lovers.

The limo drove past all the cars and pedestrians in front of the nightclub and stopped at the gate to the VIP entrance next to the nightclub. The guard at the gate recognized the limo and opened the gate for them. In the VIP parking area, a tall man dressed in a suit stood next to a bright yellow sports car. It was Mrs Jane's other lover. Unbeknownst to Mrs Jane's husband, this forty-something business owner with whom he'd done business with numerous times in the past and who he considered to be a friend, had been one of Mrs Jane's sexual boy-toys long before they'd even met.

Mrs Jane didn't wait for the chauffeur to open her door when the limo parked. When she saw her lover standing there waiting for her, she got out of the limo and called out his name. Kathy also got out of the limo and stayed close to Mrs Jane as her lover walked up to her with open arms. Seeing the two of them hugging and kissing with as much passion as a newly wed young couple, Kathy felt the burning urge to tell this lover about all the other lovers.

Kathy escorted Mrs Jane and her lover into the club through the rear entrance which led straight to the VIP area of the nightclub. There was a bar and a number of small rooms. They went into one of the rooms which had a small table and four chairs in it. The entire one side of the room was a two-way mirror which allowed them to look out at all the young people partying, dancing and drinking in the nightclub. Kathy stood in the corner of the room for the better part of two hours as the two drank and flirted with each other. She turned her head when she saw how the two began fondling with each other. They acted as if she wasn't even in the room. Showing no shame as they groped each other and as they spoke about how they were looking forward to making love. Kathy wondered if she would ever meet a man who wasn't like Mrs Jane's lovers.

When they left the nightclub, Mrs Jane's lover followed the limo in his sports car. Kathy didn't find it strange when Mrs Jane told the chauffeur to take her to her office building. There was a small storage room on the top floor of the building that had been used by Mrs Jane as a closet in the past, until she turned the room into her own little private sex playroom. The limo and sports car drove to Mrs Jane's private parking area next to the office building. When the vehicles stopped, Mrs Jane's lover got out of his car and walked up to the side of the limo as the chauffeur was opening the rear door for her. As Kathy and the assistant also got out of the limo, she began feeling that tingling sensation in her right hand again. The sensation quickly spread throughout her entire body. Kathy tried not to show that she was starting to feel dizzy. Mrs Jane handed her key card to her assistant and told him to go open the door. She kissed and groped her lover, and didn't notice how Kathy leaned against the limo to prevent herself from collapsing. Mrs Jane and her lover began walking to the open door, and when Kathy began walking after them, the dizziness became worse, she tripped and fell to the ground. Mrs Jane and her lover turned around and looked at her.

"What's wrong with you? Have you been drinking on the job?" Mrs Jane asked, showing less than zero concern for Kathy's well-being.

"Maybe she bought dope from the dealers at the nightclub. Your little bitch bodyguard could be high right now," Mrs Jane's lover chuckled mockingly.

The chauffeur and the assistant rushed to Kathy's side and helped her up. Neither of them wanted to ask, but being truly concerned for her well-being, both of them asked her if she'd been drinking, taken any illegal drugs, or if she had a medical condition of some sort.

"Thanks guys. But I'm not drunk or high. I've just been getting these dizzy spells and getting this weird feeling all over my body," she said before she shook her head and felt that the dizziness was starting to go away.

"Do you always employ weak poor nobodies to guard you?" Mrs Jane's lover asked as he stared at Kathy with a judgmental look in his eyes.

"Pathetic!" Mrs Jane said as she let go of her lover and walked up to Kathy. "I don't care what's wrong with you! I can't employ a weak little bitch who can't protect me! You're fired! Get your useless ass off my property now!"

The chauffeur and assistant let go of Kathy as she angrily stepped forward and said, "You really don't give a shit about anyone other than yourself and your man-whores, do you?"

"How dare you talk to me like I..."

"How dare I? How dare you?!" Kathy said angrily as she unleashed all the anger she'd kept bottled up inside. "How dare you fuck around behind your husband's back with every willing man who flashes a little cash and shows interest in you?!"

Mrs Jane wanted to threaten Kathy, but she paused for a moment when she thought of all the things Kathy could go tell her husband.

All of them were so caught up in the moment that none of them noticed the neon blue light flickering in the dark alleyway right across the street from the private parking area. The flickering grew brighter until there were two bright blue flashes of light, then the flickering stopped. Footsteps could be heard in the dark alleyway. Two people came walking out of the alleyway. Klouser and Xanthy began walking across the street towards the private parking area. Both in their thirties, they were armed with what they called *'gutter blades'* – strange-looking short swords with eighteen inch long blades, which had two small hook-shaped blades on the back of the blades. Klouser had bushy brown hair and Xanthy had wavy red hair. The bright streetlights that were shining on their pitch black leather pants, jackets and boots almost made it look as if they were glowing as they both pulled their gutter blades from their leather sheaths and prepared to attack.

Kathy and Mrs Jane were still busy exchanging insults and threats when the chauffeur and assistant spotted the two walking across the street. When they walked straight towards the parking area's entrance, the chauffeur raised his hand, walked up to them, and said, "You can't come in here. This is a private - "

Klouser slashed him across the chest before swinging his blade and slitting his throat. As the chauffeur collapsed, Xanthy attacked, stabbed and slashed the assistant before pushing him out of the way. Mrs Jane and her lover both screamed as they rushed to get into the back of the limo and locked the doors. The shock and panic caused by what they'd just witnessed had made them forget that the door to the office building was wide open. They would've stood a better chance of escaping if they'd entered the building and locked the door. Kathy pulled out her pistol and began firing at the two. Her bullets struck both of them in the stomach and chest. They collapsed but through the groans of pain, both chuckled. Xanthy stopped chuckling when she slowly got back up, looked at her shirt and jacket, and said, "You just ruined my favorite outfit, you stupid little slut!"

When Klouser also got back up, Kathy opened fire on them both again and emptied her pistol on them. Her bullets struck them and appeared to hurt them, but why wouldn't they just die? Were they perhaps wearing body armor underneath their clothes? As Kathy rushed to reload her pistol, Mrs Jane slowly opened the limo's rear door and peaked out. Hearing the gunshots made her think that Kathy had killed the two attackers. She saw Klouser and Xanthy slowly getting back on their feet, and saw Kathy reloading her pistol. She foolishly decided to make a run for the door. Mrs Jane's lover followed her as she got out of the limo and made a run for the door to the building. Klouser threw his gutter blade, sending it spinning through the air, missing Kathy's head by mere inches. The blade struck Mrs Jane in the back, tearing through her loveless heart and killing her instantly.

"Noooo!" her lover screamed in horror as her dead body hit the ground.

Kathy opened fire on them again just as Xanthy threw her blade at the crying lover who dropped down on his knees next to Mrs Jane's body. Her blade struck him in the side of his head, splitting his skull in half. Kathy shot them again before she looked back over her shoulder and saw the two dead bodies. Shocked by what she was witnessing, she couldn't believe her eyes when she saw the dim blue glow coming from the two gutter blades. Both blood covered blades tore out of the two dead bodies before they flew through the air on their own. Kathy tried to dodge the blades. One of them slashed the shoulder of her jacket as it flew past her. Klouser and Xanthy, who were pointing the glowing palms of their hands at the blades, caught their blades and began walking towards her. Kathy fired the last bullets in her pistol at them, tossed the empty pistol at Klouser's head, turned back and began running. After dodging the pistol, Klouser yelled, "Yes! Run! That's all that your alternate selves could do too!"

Kathy wouldn't have run if these two didn't appear to be unstoppable. She was well trained in hand to hand combat. The training she'd done in different forms of martial arts in the two years before she'd become a full time bodyguard made her more dangerous than the average guy who knew how to swing a few punches. Even if Klouser and Xanthy hadn't been armed with gutter blades, she didn't want to risk taking them on in a fist fight when her bullets clearly didn't hurt them. She ran across the empty parking area behind the office building until she reached the backstreet behind the building. She began running down the sidewalk too afraid to look back.

Klouser and Xanthy walked across the parking area with their blades in hand. When they reached the backstreet and saw Kathy running in the distance, Klouser sighed and said, "Ah dammit. Looks like yet another game of cat and mouse."

"Meow-meow," Xanthy said before she and Klouser began running after her.

Kathy looked back over her shoulder and saw the two running after her. She ran across the street to the nearest alleyway. There was barely enough light in the long dirty alleyway for her to see where she was running. She was making her way through all the garbage that was scattered in the alleyway when she heard the footsteps behind her. She looked back and saw Klouser and Xanthy running towards her. As she continued running, she saw someone ahead running straight at her. The first thought in her mind was that it was also someone who wanted to kill her – perhaps someone who worked with Klouser and Xanthy. Klouser pointed his hand at the trashcans along the side of the alleyway. The palm of his hand glowed bright blue and he used his powers to move the trashcans. Kathy was struck by two trashcans and knocked off her feet. She fell between the garbage on the ground between the trashcans. As she was getting up, she saw four trashcans – all of which were glowing dim blue – flying through the air past her. Klouser and Xanthy tried to use their powers to knock the trashcans out of the air, but only managed to do so with two of them. The other two trashcans struck them and knocked them off their feet. Just as Kathy was back on her feet and was about to continue running, the other stranger who she'd seen running towards her grabbed her by her forearm, and said, "Come with me. Run."

She tried to pull her arm free, tried to punch him, and screamed, "Let me go!"

"Kathy! Kathy! Stop fighting and follow me!" he said as he let go of her arm. She looked back at Klouser and Xanthy before looking at the stranger again. He'd taken a step away from her to show her that he didn't want to hurt her. He held out his hand to her and yelled, "Come on, Rosebud! Come with me! I'll protect you!"

She grabbed his hand and the two of them ran together to the other side of the alleyway. They ran down another backstreet.

There were two vagrants who were looking for anything to eat in the trashcans behind a convenience store. Two cops who were patrolling the streets in the neighborhood came out of a small abandoned building and were walking towards their patrol car. A pedestrian who was walking down the street – a down on his luck, recently unemployed young man who'd just been kicked out of the apartment he and his girlfriend shared because he lost his job – had a small bag of his belongings in his hand and tears in his eyes.

Kathy and the stranger ran past all of them. The two cops wanted to stop them and ask them why they were running, but then they heard more footsteps heading their way and saw Klouser and Xanthy running down the middle of the street. Also seeing them coming, the two vagrants stepped in front of Klouser and Xanthy to stop them and ask for spare change. Both of them swung their gutter blades at the vagrants as they ran past them and mortally wounded them. One was slashed across the throat and the other was slashed across the side of his neck. As both vagrants collapsed, the two cops pulled out their guns and ran towards Klouser and Xanthy yelling at them to drop their weapons. The pedestrian dropped his bag and stumbled before freezing in a state of shock as he stared at the two dying vagrants. The cops ran after them and again yelled at them to stop and drop their blades when Klouser and Xanthy stopped running and looked back at the cops. The pedestrian ran up to the cops, yelling in a state of panic, "You guys have to do something! Those two bums are dying over there!"

Klouser and Xanthy pointed their glowing hands at the cops and used their powers to pull their guns out of their hands and to send them flying through the air. Instead of just attacking the three with their gutter blades and killing them as they easily could have done, they attacked them and fought with them. The pedestrian was knocked down and left dazed with only two blows to the face. The cops put up more of a fight but they also weren't really a match for them. Klouser and Xanthy punched and kicked them until they were down on the ground. Xanthy was preparing to finish them off with her blade when she saw Klouser pulling a small leather bag out of his jacket's breast pocket.

"Oh come on! We don't have time for drones. Let's just kill them and go finish off Kathy! We're wasting time! They're getting away," Xanthy said, sounding impatient and somewhat agitated.

"They could be heading anywhere right now. We need a few drones to help us catch them. They could be heading for a hot spot as we speak," Klouser said as he took three small strange-looking devices out of his leather bag.

The small diamond-shaped metal device had a thin needle on it with a wire wrapped around the needle – the wire was so thin that it was virtually invisible to the naked eye – and a small glowing red light on the back of it. Xanthy helped Klouser hold the two cops and the pedestrian down as he stuck one of these devices in the back of each of their necks. All three of them appeared to have some sort of seizure as the device took control of their minds. The three finally became silent, got up and stood in front of Klouser and Xanthy like obedient slaves awaiting orders from their masters. The devices had turned all three of them into mindless drones ready to do whatever they were told to do. The colors of their eyes changed from blue and brown to red.

"The two other planewalkers who we're hunting are on the run," Klouser told them. Thanks to the devices controlling their minds, each of the three drones saw images of Kathy and the stranger who helped her appear in front of them when Klouser mentioned their names.

"Hunt them and fight them with everything you've got. Try to hurt them as much as possible."

The pedestrian drone and the two cop drones ran down the street and began their hunt. Xanthy pulled Klouser closer and kissed him before she said, "I hope your plan works. You know I don't like turning these dumb normal people into drones. Sometimes they just get in the way."

"We have to do everything we can to catch the last and original version of Kathy. Just because we've come this far doesn't mean we should stop giving our mission our all."

They put their gutter blades back in their sheaths and ran down the street.

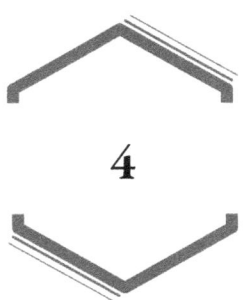

4

Kathy and the handsome stranger ran down a narrow alleyway. She was struggling to keep up with him. They ran out of the alleyway into a quiet street. There were only a few cars driving up and down the street, and a group of three men and one woman who were walking home after a night out at a nearby bar. The stranger looked around before pulling on Kathy's hand and saying, "This way. There's a portal hot spot here somewhere. I can feel it."

He saw how she kept touching her shoulder and noticed that it was bleeding.

"Don't worry about that. It might hurt like hell now but the pain will go away and your healing will start to speed up as you start to gain your powers. Just stick with me to protect you, and stay strong Rosebud."

Out of breath, scared and confused, Kathy asked, "Who are... you? What... powers? And... how do you... know my nickname? Only my..."

"Only your parents used to call you that. I know."

Hearing him say that left her speechless. She hadn't told anyone about what her parents called her when they were still alive. How could he possibly know this?

"My name is Trent. You'll probably start remembering me soon. Or at least remember seeing me."

Kathy was too out of breath to reply. She felt like she had a hundred questions she wanted to ask him but didn't know where to start. They ran from one street to the next though a number of alleyways and side streets. They finally came to a stop in front of a small bookstore in a backstreet. Kathy was too out of breath, too afraid and confused to continue running until Trent answered a few of her questions. She opened her mouth to speak but couldn't. She was still busy catching her breath when she took a closer look at Trent. The light above the bookstore's door was bright enough for her to see his face. She stared at him as if she was staring at a ghost. She remembered his face, every little detail of his face seemed familiar to her. As if she'd seen him before, touched his face before, ran her fingers through his hair before, and kissed him before, but why couldn't she remember.

"You... your face. Your... name. I... remember you. And the two who... attacked me. I remember them too," was all she managed to say before she leaned back against the bookstore's door and wiped the sweat from her forehead.

"Those two are Klouser and Xanthy. They want to kill you for your powers."

Hearing him say their names made her gasp as she remembered something. The nightmares she'd been having where she kept seeing herself being killed by a man and a woman, she remembered the faces of the man and woman as she'd seen them in her nightmares and she was sure that they were Klouser and Xanthy.

"I saw them... in my dreams," she paused as she stared at Trent's face again. "You too. I've seen you in my dreams too."

When Trent opened his mouth to speak, he paused and something strange happened to his eyes. A faint blue glow flickered and moved around the outer edges of his eyes.

"Come on. We have to keep moving and find the portal hot spot. They're getting closer."

He took her by the hand and they continued running. As everything Trent had just told her kept playing on a loop in her mind, this only added to Kathy's fear and confusion. To make matters worse, she could feel the tingling sensations all over her body and she feared that she might become dizzy again. Holding on to her hand as they ran, Trent could feel her hand start to shake. He could feel her tightening her grip on his hand as she tried as hard as she could to fight through the strange sensations she was feeling throughout her entire body.

"Don't fight it," he said. "Your body is trying to resist your powers. Just let go and let it start flowing through your body and mind."

How could she possibly relax at a time like this? How could she just let these strange sensations move through her body and trust that it wouldn't harm her in some or other way? It took a lot of effort from her to try and relax. For more than ten minutes, her body still tried to resist the strange sensations. It was only when she grew too tired, and felt too physically drained from all the running, that her body and mind lowered their resistance against the sensations. The tingling sensations instantly intensified. She felt burning sensations followed by cold spots all over her body. It felt as if every muscle, every nerve, and every drop of blood in her body was being overwhelmed by the clash of hot and cold sensations throughout her entire body.

They reached yet another backstreet. When Trent slowed down, Kathy thought that he was also starting to feel tired from all the running, but that wasn't the case. She noticed that he kept looking around as they ran. Fearing that Klouser and Xanthy might have caught up with them, she also looked around but saw nobody. They continued running down the backstreet for less than a minute before Trent pointed at a chain-link fence ahead, and said, "Over there."

When they reached the fence, Kathy saw the big construction site on the other side of the fence. Trent pulled out one of his gutter blades and the cutting edge of its blade glowed as he swung it a few times and slashed a hole in the fence.

"Stay close," he said before he led her through the hole to the construction site. Neither of them saw the two cop drones. Having seen them climbing through the hole in the fence, the two cop drones ran towards the fence. Klouser, Xanthy and the pedestrian drone came running around the corner and saw the cop drones running straight to the construction site. They ran after them and caught up with them just as they stopped in front of the hole in the fence. Klouser and Xanthy's eyes briefly glowed bright blue as they looked at the construction site.

"Shit! A portal hot spot," Xanthy said. "We have to get them before they escape."

Trent was leading Kathy through the dimly lit construction site. To her it felt as if they were moving through a maze. As they moved between the building materials, dump trucks, pickup trucks, and concrete mixers, she wondered if Trent knew where he was going or if they were going in circles. Trent could feel her grip on his hand tighten when they heard the sound of footsteps behind them.

Klouser and Xanthy were leading the three drones through the maze. They kept looking around but saw no sign of Kathy and Trent. They could sense that the two were close. They walked past a pickup truck and continued walking towards more piles of building materials and looked for the two there. Fearing that Kathy and Trent might be hiding somewhere and waiting for a chance to escape, Klouser told the drones to split up and search for them.

Kathy and Trent were hiding behind that pickup truck. Knowing that their lives were in danger, and fearing that whatever was going on inside of her body might cause her to faint or collapse while they ran from their pursuers, Kathy looked at Trent. He could feel her body trembling and could see the fear in her eyes. He looked around, pointed his blade at the narrow path between two dump trucks, squeezed her hand, and whispered in her ear, "This way. Don't let go of my hand, no matter what."

She and Trent quietly moved down the narrow path between the two dump trucks. He could sense the portal hot spot was close. As they moved from between the dump trucks to behind a small trailer where some tools were stored in, Kathy saw the site's main entrance gate. She saw that there wasn't any barbwire on top of the locked gate.

She wanted to run and try to escape by climbing over the gate before anyone saw her, but when she tried to run, Trent pulled her back and whispered angrily, "Don't try to run. If they see you, you're as good as dead. Stay with me."

She wanted to reply, but he quickly covered her mouth with his hand and shook his head. He paused as the blue glow in his eyes briefly flickered. He looked to his left and began leading her towards a pickup truck that was parked close to the fence. Four feet to the left of the pickup was a big pile of bricks. Trent looked back to see if anyone had seen them before he put his blade back in its sheath. His eyes and the palm of his hand began to glow as he pointed his hand at the area between the pickup and the pile of bricks. Kathy couldn't believe her eyes when she saw the dimly glowing blue circle appear between the pickup and the bricks. As the circle grew bigger, she saw nothing but pitch black nothing in it. He was busy opening a portal. The glowing circle quickly grew bigger until it changed shape into a rectangle. That was when Kathy began seeing moving colors in the pitch black nothing. The moving colors she saw were millions of ones and zeros. A binary code. Most of the ones and zeros were bright blue, but there were also a few clearly visible bright pink ones as well. Trent pulled her by the hand and they began running straight towards the open portal. At that moment, one of the cop drones spotted them, pulled out his firearm and began shooting at them. Hearing this, Klouser, Xanthy and the other two drones came running. One of the cop drone's bullets struck Kathy in her right forearm just as she and Trent leaped into the open portal and disappeared between all the ones and zeros.

"Quickly! Before it closes! Jump in!" Klouser shouted as he and Xanthy ran towards the portal. Both of them pointed their glowing hands at the portal to try and keep it open, but it was too late. The portal closed and disappeared before they could reach it or use their powers to keep it open a little longer. Furious that they'd gotten away, Klouser and Xanthy took their anger out on the drones. They yelled at the drones for not stopping them from escaping, and Xanthy punched two of them to relieve her anger and frustration. She was about to take a swing at the third drone with her blade when Klouser stopped her and told her that they didn't have any time to waste. Both of them pointed their hands at the spot where the portal had opened and used their powers to open it again. The two held hands as they jumped into the portal, followed by the three drones.

CHAPTER II

1

Silence. The beautiful red clouds in the sky created by a perfect sunset. The mountains, hills and sand dunes all around seemed never-ending. The desolation created a peaceful atmosphere. There was absolutely no signs of life to be seen anywhere. No birds in the sky and no people or animals on the ground. To most, this sunset would look so perfectly beautiful that one would think that such a sight would only be seen once in a lifetime. But the sunset, the clouds in the sky and everything on the ground always remained the same. This was the Transition Plane.

For any planewalker who found a portal hot spot in the Prime Physical Plane, or opened a portal in whatever other plane they found themselves in, if a planewalker wanted to move from one plane to the next, they always had to travel through the Transition Plane first.

Between the dark dunes, the sand swirled as bolts of lightning began flashing above the ground. The lightning bolts grew brighter and flashed faster as a glowing neon blue doorway – a portal – appeared in the ball of bright blue light that the lightning bolts were forming. The lines of blue and pink ones and zeros inside the open portal kept moving in opposite directions. Kathy and Trent came leaping out through the open portal. Hand in hand, their bodies stopped in mid-air and were frozen in what appeared to be a state of suspended animation. The portal behind them closed and vanished without a trace. Together, they looked like a 3D portrait of two lovers running for their lives: their knuckles were pale from how tightly they were gripping each other's hand, the expression on Kathy's face was one of fear and shock while the expression on Trent's face was one of determination and rage. The drops of blood which came from the wound on Kathy's right forearm hovered next to her arm. Although she couldn't move or speak in her frozen state, she could see what was in front of her, she could feel the pain from her wound and she could feel Trent's hand gripping hers. Trent also couldn't move or speak in his frozen state, but having been a planewalker for so many years, he could move his eyes. He kept looking down.

On the ground beneath them, the sand and dust began moving. It appeared as if five small twisters were forming beneath them. The sand and dust briefly moved violently in these five spots until five ghost-like figures emerged from out of the ground. They were the five Guardians of the Transition Plane. No-one knew if they were ghosts, spirits, angels, or demons. And no planewalker ever understood why the Guardians always did the same thing every time a planewalker moved from one plane of existence to the next. The Guardians appeared to be in spirit form. They were partially transparent. The parts of them that were visible looked both angelic and demonic at the same time. The one that was leading the others up towards Kathy and Trent appeared to have the face of a little boy and had long curly hair. His body was covered in pieces of a torn robe. The second Guardian looked like the spirit of an old woman. Her hair looked like hundreds of butterfly wings, and her body was covered in a cloak that was covered in strange symbols and numbers. The third Guardian looked like the spirit of a barbarian. He had a long beard and his body was covered in armor. The fourth Guardian looked like a young girl with long straight hair and big eyes. Her body was covered with a robe made of flowers and leaves. The last Guardian looked like an old bald man with torn pieces of different fabrics covering his body.

The Guardians flew up to Kathy and Trent and began flying around them in circles. All five of them made strange noises before they began flying through Kathy and Trent from different angles over and over again. They kept flying faster and faster until they faded into what looked like one big white blur of light. Kathy could feel them moving through her body over and over again. The feeling was indescribable. Suddenly, the Guardians flew out of their bodies and flew up into the air. They hovered above Kathy and Trent as they pointed their fingers at the open area in front of the two. On the ground, bolts of lightning shot out of so many spots all at once. At every single spot where there had been a bolt of lightning, a short glowing blue line appeared on the ground. The Guardians waved their hands at the ground which caused portals to appear out of the ground where some – not all – of these blue lines were. Each open portal looked like a glowing blue door frame with the moving blue and pink ones and zeros clearly visible in each of them. The Guardians pointed their hands at Kathy and Trent and used their powers to move them through the air in their suspended state towards the open portals. It appeared as if the Guardians were trying to pick which open portal to send them through. Kathy and Trent were being moved from one open portal to the next until they were finally moved into one of the portals in the middle and their bodies vanished into it. The Guardians all let out what sounded like a combination of an angelic cry and a demonic growl. In the blink of an eye, all the portals disappeared back into the ground.

The Guardians were moving down and were about to vanish back into the ground when the portal door through which Kathy and Trent had entered the Transition Plane opened again. They paused and stared at the portal until Klouser and Xanthy came through the portal. Hand in hand, their bodies hovered in mid-air in a state of suspended animation. The three drones also came through the portal one by one. The Guardians moved through Klouser and Xanthy like they did with Kathy and Trent. When they moved on to the drones, the Guardians seemed skeptical. They knew these three weren't planewalkers. It was only after moving through the bodies of the drones that they sensed the three were being controlled by the devices in the back of their necks. They knew these devices well. Many evil planewalkers in the past had also used these devices to create temporary slaves out of normal humans. Like Kathy and Trent, Klouser and Xanthy were sent into one open portal while each of the three drones were sent into separate portals. Those who hold hands while going into the Transition Plane are sent to the same plane, whereas all those who aren't holding hands with their companions are sent to different planes.

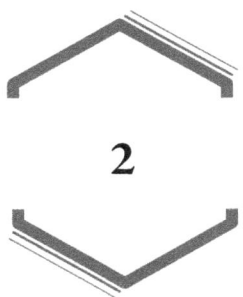

2

It was night in the big city. On the south side of the city, close to the low cost housing projects, there was a graveyard. Unlike the big city cemetery on the east side, this graveyard looked like it was forgotten by most. One could easily tell by the state of the graveyard and the state of the small church next to it that this was where the poorest of the poor were laid to rest. The church building on the outside was covered in graffiti. So too were many of the headstones in the graveyard. In the middle of the graveyard, between all the headstones, there was a mausoleum. It wasn't the mausoleum of a wealthy or famous person or family. One could tell by the look of it from the outside that it had been built with the cheapest materials available, and by people who didn't have the building skills to make it a proper mausoleum. It was the mausoleum of the James family. Like everyone else on the south side, the James family was poor. Being a close family, their grandfather had decided that they needed a mausoleum to keep the ashes of their deceased family members together.

On the outside of the mausoleum, the wooden door was covered with graffiti. There was something else on the door as well. Underneath all the spray paint, there was a crest. One of the family members had tried to carve the James family crest into the door years back, but that could hardly be seen anymore. Inside of the mausoleum, there were four shelves on two of the walls. Some shelves were still empty whereas the others had the urns containing the ashes of members of the James family on them. On one wall, there was a large mirror that covered almost the entire wall. On the mirror were small photographs of every deceased family member with the date of death written on it. All of the photographs fell from the mirror as its surface appeared to turn into some sort of liquid. The metal frame of the mirror began glowing neon blue as the entire mirror turned pitch black before the glowing ones and zeroes began appearing on it. The portal opened. Kathy and Trent came through the portal. Still holding each other by the hand, their bodies struck the shelves on the opposite wall, breaking some of the shelves. As their bodies hit the floor, urns, ashes and pieces of the broken shelves fell on them. Kathy screamed as she let go of Trent's hand and began swinging her fists. It was too dark inside the mausoleum for her to see anything. In as much pain as she was, her mind and body were in survival mode. Trent tried to calm her down.

"Kathy! Hold on! Stop! You're safe! Calm down! We are – " was all he said before he was punched on the cheek. In her state of panic, she'd accidentally punched him. Left dizzy by her punch, he still tried to grab her hands. He received two more blows to the chest before he managed to grab hold of her wrists.

"Let go! Get away from me!" she screamed as she continued to fight him.

"Let me help you!"

She continued to resist until he pulled her close, let go of her wrists, and hugged her. She wanted to push him away but the way he held her made her feel safe. She couldn't fathom how or why but the way in which he held her, the feeling of his arms around her and his chin pressing against her shoulder made her feel safe. For some reason, the feeling of her in his arms awakened a memory, a familiar feeling of complete safety. Part of her still wanted to push him away and demand answers from him, while part of her just wanted him to hold her and never let go. The mixed emotions in her confused, fear-filled mind were interrupted by pain. As Trent held her, he was unknowingly pressing against her wounded right forearm.

"My... my..." was all she managed to say, but she didn't have to say more. Trent could tell by the sound of her voice that she was in pain. He let go of her, got up, made his way to the door and tried to open it, but it was locked. He rammed it with his shoulder until the cheap lock broke and the door swung open. When he helped Kathy up so that they could leave, she tried to ask him a few of the many questions she had. All that she managed to ask was, "We... we... What place was that? Why... why couldn't we move? Who are you? And... how do... you know me? Why do those two... want to kill...me? Where are – ?"

She stopped speaking and pressed her wounded forearm against her chest, pressing on the wound with her left hand to try and stop the bleeding. Besides this pain, she could feel a burning pain in certain areas of her body and numbness in other areas. She could almost still feel the Guardians moving through her body.

"A planewalker's first trip through the Transition Plane is always a painful one. Don't worry about that. It gets better."

Through her pain, fear, and confusion, hearing what Trent was saying made her think for a moment that he was mad. Nothing he was saying made sense to her. But remembering what she'd seen with her own eyes, she knew that her best bet for surviving whatever the hell was going on was to trust him. She took him by the hand with her bloody left hand and followed him out of the mausoleum. They made their way through the graveyard in the dark to the church. There was a light above the wooden cross on the wall next to the entrance doors. Trent kept looking around as he led her to the light. Kathy leaned against the wall. She kept her wounded arm against her body, too afraid to see how bad the wound was. Trent touched her hand and said, "Let me take a look at it." She hesitated briefly before turning her head, clenching her teeth, and whispering, "How bad is it?", before showing him her arm. He slowly and gently pulled up her sleeve and looked at the wound. She was waiting for him to say something like, *'Oh my God! We have to get you to a hospital!'* Imagine her shock when she heard him say, "It doesn't look that bad. You're healing up quicker than others who haven't fully ascended yet."

His words left her shaking her head in disbelief. What was he talking about? His words didn't shock her as much as his tone did. To her, it sounded as if he was speaking about her bullet wound as if it was a paper cut. She hesitated but slowly opened her eyes and looked at her arm. The wound wasn't bleeding that much anymore. Her left hand shook as she touched the wound with her fingertip. She felt almost no pain anymore. The wound slowly began healing and closing right before her eyes.

"Hurts and it takes a little longer than normal to heal, but you'll heal quicker once you have all your powers. Don't worry, Rosebud. I'll stick with you and protect you from those two while you ascend," Trent said.

Kathy opened her mouth to speak but paused. It felt to her as if all the questions she wanted to ask him wanted to flood out of her mouth all at once.

"How do you know what my parents used to call me? They were the only ones who called me that."

"You told me. Well, not this you. One of your alternate selves told me."

What Trent was saying made no sense to her whatsoever. This only added to her confusion. Trent kept looking at her healing wound. When he looked her straight in the eye and opened his mouth to speak, he paused. Kathy was too confused by it all to notice the way he was looking at her, and what he did next only added to the list of questions she had to ask him: he pulled her closer and hugged her.

"What are you doing?! Get back!"

Trent apologized as he let go of her. Kathy felt overwhelmed by everything. Instead of letting all her fears and confusion get to her, she took a deep breath, looked at her healing wound, looked at him, and asked, "What is happening to me? And don't tell me like I already know anything about what's going on because I don't know a fucking thing!"

Trent held out his hand. This was his way of asking her: *'Do you trust me?'* She looked down at his hand, looked up at him, took him by the hand and squeezed it hard.

"You are ascending and becoming a planewalker. You and I are two of – as far as I know – the only four remaining planewalkers still alive. We unplugged so many of the others that I we believe there are no more out there."

"We? Unplugged? What do you mean by *'unplugged'* them?" Kathy asked. "Wait a minute. By *'we'*, do you mean you and those two other freaks?"

Trent sighed and it appeared as if he hung his head in shame.

"Planewalkers can't be killed like normal people. Things like bullets hurt us, but we survive and heal. There's only one way a planewalker can be killed and it's kinda tricky and messy. First we gotta cut on the back of the – "

"Hold on. Before you go on, tell me... were you with those two freaks?"

"Freaks. What an understatement," he said before he looked down at the ground in shame. "I was. A long time ago. They tracked me down shortly after I started ascending. All of it, the powers, the feeling of being almost invincible, it all scared the shit out of me at first. Klouser and Xanthy took me and began teaching me everything they knew about the powers. They made me feel like they were my family, but all they wanted from me was train me to be a killer, to be their lackey, to help them hunt down my alternate selves, and every other planewalker we could find."

While Trent spoke to her, memories came flooding through his mind of some of the many planewalkers he had helped Klouser and Xanthy hunt down and kill. He remembered every single one he'd helped to kill. He would've done anything to try and forget all the innocent lives he'd helped them to take, but his conscience wouldn't let him. Of all the planewalkers they'd killed, there were six that haunted him more than all the others. These were the ones that gave him nightmares. He could still remember their faces and the sounds of their screams as he told Kathy what he'd done:

EVERY TIME TRENT HAD a flashback of the most brutal killings that he'd taken part in, the one he always remembered first happened in an open field outside a city. He, Klouser and Xanthy were running after a female planewalker who'd gained some control over her powers, after the killer trio had killed all of her alternate selves. After Trent finally caught up with her, he grabbed her and she put up one hell of a fight. While he fought with her, Klouser and Xanthy attacked her from behind. Trent could still see the despair in her fear-filled hazel eyes right before Klouser slashed the back of her neck open, slashed her back open straight down the middle, and Xanthy unplugged her.

Not long after this killing, the killer trio were fighting an older male planewalker on top of a skyscraper. Also armed with a gutter blade, this planewalker was much more skilled in fighting. He fought off all three of them for more than twenty minutes before Trent managed to injure him. Xanthy then attacked him from behind, slashed his neck and back open, and unplugged him.

They once fought another powerful planewalker in an empty parking lot one cold December night. This one was fairly weak in comparison to many others they'd killed. Not having ascended fully yet, the twenty-something planewalker never really stood a chance against them, yet he still fought them with everything he had in him. By the time they finally unplugged him, his upper body, arms and hands were covered in cuts.

On a windy, cloudy autumn day on a small secluded beach, Trent and Klouser were fighting a planewalker who they'd been hunting for weeks. As they fought, Xanthy kept walking in circles around them, looking for the perfect opportunity to attack him from behind. When she finally attacked him and slashed the back of his neck, he turned around and slashed her across the stomach. This made Klouser go mad with rage. He attacked the planewalker and savagely slashed and stabbed him before he unplugged him.

Spring of the following year, they tracked down a female planewalker in a small suburb. When they attacked her in her living room, they underestimated her fighting abilities and how much control she'd gained over her powers. Besides fighting the three with her gutter blade, she used almost every item of furniture in her living room as a weapon. In the middle of the fight, she used her telekinetic powers to send an armchair flying through the air straight at Trent. It struck him straight from the front and sent him through a large window. She was about to use her powers to send a couch straight at Xanthy when Klouser attacked her, stabbed her, slashed her, and unplugged her.

The last haunting memory that Trent shared with Kathy was of a young male planewalker they attacked on a small cattle ranch. It was the first attack on another planewalker that he'd taken part in after Klouser and Xanthy took him under their dark wing to help them hunt down and kill all the others like them. He told her in detail how Klouser and Xanthy tortured this planewalker when he was too injured to fight back. They used this planewalker to teach Trent how to kill (unplug) a planewalker. He was ordered to slash the back of this bleeding young man's neck open. After doing so, they told him to use the hook-shaped blades on the back of his gutter blade to slash his back open, straight down along the spine. The most gruesome part of unplugging a planewalker was the part in which one ripped the intended victim's spinal column loose from his skull. While trying to do so, Trent struggled. By that time, he hadn't gained full control over all of his powers, including the enhanced physical strength that all planewalkers gained once they had fully ascended. Klouser and Xanthy kept yelling at him to try harder, mocking him, calling him a *'weakling'* until he finally ripped part of that planewalker's spinal column loose and unplugged him. Strange misty white and blue beams of light came out of the dead planewalker's body and entered Trent, Klouser and Xanthy's bodies. Their bodies hovered a foot above the ground as they absorbed the dead planewalker's powers.

Listening to Trent as he opened up to her and told her all of this in gory detail, Kathy couldn't hide her shock and disgust. In the back of her mind, she thought he was brave to confess such horrific acts to her, but as she stared at him, she began to look at him as if he was a monster. A heartless killer. She slowly stepped back. She was considering making a run for it. He was still busy talking about how much he regretted all the lives he took while he worked for Klouser and Xanthy, when he noticed how she was slowly turning away from him. She was looking across the road, looking for a path to take to run away from him. Just as she moved her right foot and was on the verge of running away, he grabbed her by her arm.

"Please don't – "

Kathy tried to pull her arm free and began putting up a fight.

"Nooo! Let go! Let go of me! You're a monster!" she yelled as she began hitting his hand, trying to free her arm from his grip. "You've got the wrong woman! Let go!"

"I – I know I was a monster! But I – "

She continued to put up a fight. During their struggle, he tried as hard as he could to keep her from running away without harming her in any way. He pulled her closer to him and when she looked at him, she could see tears in his eyes. Her survival instinct was telling her to fight him with all she had in her and run away, but seeing the look in his eyes made her pause for a moment.

"Yes, I was a bad guy. Yes, I – I did things that I regret. Things that haunt me. Things that I would never have considered doing if I hadn't followed Klouser and Xanthy. And, yes, I killed planewalkers and their alternate selves for their powers. But thanks to… thanks to someone who opened my eyes, someone who made me realize how bad those two were, I turned against them. Why do you think I saved your ass?"

Hearing all this added to Kathy's confusion. She could feel him loosening his grip on her arm. When she stopped struggling, he let go of her arm and took two steps back to show her that he wasn't going to harm her.

"If you worked with those two freaks, what made you turn against them and what made you come to help me?"

Trent opened his mouth to answer her, took a deep breath, paused before he exhaled and turned his head to look at the road.

"That's not important. You don't need to know that now. All you need to know is that we have to keep you safe. Those two have had their powers much longer than me. If I could take them on alone and defeat them to protect you, I would. Best we can do now is keep moving and keep you safe until you ascend completely and gain full control over your powers."

She stepped closer to him, gently put her fingers on the side of his chin and turned his head towards her. Looking straight into his eyes, she put on a brave face and said, "I'm listening. Tell me more. Sounds like there's a lot I need to know."

He took her by the hand, kissed her fingers, and smiled as he said, "Finally. A little cooperation."

"Tell me everything you can think of as quick as you can. We don't know when those two will track us down," she said as she took a quick look around to make sure they were alone.

"You've been having strange feelings, pains in your body. You got dizzy for no reason. You've been having nightmares where you see yourself being killed."

Hearing Trent say this made her remember seeing Klouser and Xanthy in the nightmares she had in which she kept seeing herself being killed. She was about to tell him this when he said something that left her even more confused.

"The pains and strange feelings in your body were a sign that you were gaining more and more of your powers. Every time Klouser and Xanthy killed one of your alternate selves in one of the alternate physical planes, their powers came straight to you."

Kathy shook her head as she said, "But... but you just told me about how you three killed other planewalkers and took their powers."

"We first killed all their alternate selves on all the alternate physical planes. If you kill all of a planewalker's alternate selves on the other planes, that planewalker on the Prime Physical Plane gains all of the powers and knowledge, but only gains access to that knowledge and control over those powers when he or she fully ascends."

"I don't have any powers yet."

Trent smiled as he looked at her. He took her hand and placed it against his mouth. She didn't have a clue what he was trying to show her until she heard his voice in her head saying, "One of the first powers you usually gain control over is telepathy. It's creepy at first, and it won't save your ass in a fight, but it's still useful."

Kathy pulled her hand away from his mouth, and asked, "What the fuck are you doing in my head?"

"It's not so creepy once you've used that power a few times. You've still got so much to learn."

Trent put his arms around her and gave her a hug. She quickly pushed him away, and said, "Hold on there. You're telling me that the two of us and those two freaks aren't human?"

"All of us are human. We're just not normal humans," he replied.

"Define normal."

Trent took her by the hand and led her back into the grave yard.

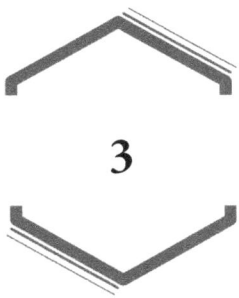

3

In the Transition Plane, the portal door opened again, and Klouser and Xanthy came leaping through it. Their bodies froze in mid-air and the Guardians came out of the ground to do what they did to all planewalkers every time they traveled through the Transition Plane. Having searched for Kathy and Trent on another plane, they didn't care to how many planes they had to travel to hunt them both down and kill them.

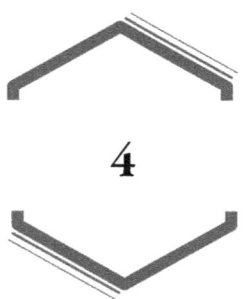

4

Trent took Kathy to a dark path between two rows of graves. He kept pointing his dimly glowing hand around until it began glowing a little brighter. They stopped next to the grave of a little boy close to the mausoleum.

"Hold out your hand," Trent said.

Kathy held out her hand and felt like a fool at first because nothing was happening. Everything he'd done with his powers so far made it look easy. For a moment, she began doubting whether she truly had all these so-called powers that he claimed a planewalker normally had.

"Why isn't anything happening?" she asked.

"You don't just snap your fingers and ascend completely. You gain some of your powers and knowledge bit by bit," he said.

Standing behind her, Trent put his arms around Kathy's waist, and whispered in her ear, "On the Prime Physical Plane, there are portal hot spots. In some cities, they're almost around every corner, and in others there are only a handful. On all the alternate physical planes, you can open a portal almost anywhere, or you can use any big mirror to open a portal."

Pointing her open hand out in front of her, she could sense something in front of her. She stared at the empty dark path in front of her, saw absolutely nothing there, yet something inside of her sensed that there was something there.

"Do you feel it yet?" he asked.

"I... I feel something."

He put his hands on her hips, squeezed gently, and said, "Concentrate. There's a portal right in front of you. Imagine your life is in danger and you have to escape. How badly do you want to open that portal door and escape?"

Kathy imagined herself being chased by an army of men armed with swords and knives. She could feel a tingling sensation move through her body, through her arm to her hand. Her eyes began to glow as a dim glow began flickering in the middle of the palm of her hand. A dim glowing blue line appeared in the ground in front of her. She felt a burning sensation in her hand as the outer edges of the glowing blue portal door began to appear in front of her.

"You're doing it. Just try harder," he said.

She smiled as the portal door began taking shape in front of her and she could see a few dimly glowing ones and zeroes. At that very moment, they saw a flash of blue light coming from inside the mausoleum.

The mirror's frame inside the mausoleum glowed as the portal opened. Klouser and Xanthy came through the open portal and their bodies landed on what remained of the shelves and urns.

Trent grabbed Kathy by the hand, pointed his other hand at the portal door she was busy opening and used his powers to open it completely. He began running towards it, pulling her along, and yelled, "They found us! Come on!" before they jumped into the open portal.

Seconds later, Klouser and Xanthy came out of the mausoleum and saw the portal door vanishing back into the ground. She banged her fist against the side of the mausoleum out of sheer frustration. He grabbed her by the hand and said, "Come. Let's go through the same portal door. Maybe the Guardians will send us to whatever plane they're going to send them."

They ran towards the spot where the portal door had just closed and used their powers to open it again. After they vanished into the portal door, it remained open for a brief moment before it slowly began to close. Once it had vanished back into the ground and the blue afterglow slowly faded away, the tranquil darkness and silence of night returned to the graveyard.

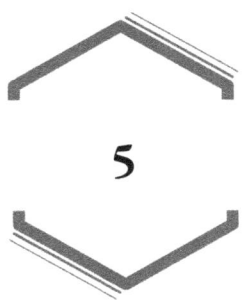

5

In the middle of a desert, a rattlesnake was making its way across the long dusty road. Just as it made its way in between a few big rocks next to the road, bolts of lightning shot out of the road and a portal door opened. Kathy and Trent came leaping out through the portal. They kept gripping each other by the hand as they both stumbled and fell in the middle of the road. As the portal closed, she curled up in agony. The painful burning sensations she felt throughout her body felt ten times worse than it had felt before. Tears dripped from her eyes. She opened her mouth to call out to Trent for help but she was in too much pain to make a sound. She felt him squeeze her hand and heard him saying something but, to her, it just sounded like muffled gibberish. He didn't let go of her hand as he stood on his knees next to her. When her body began to shake, he placed his other hand under her head. He could see the neon blue light dimly flickering in her eyes. Dim blue glowing spots began appearing on her body. They began moving around in random directions all over her body, glowing brighter and brighter as they moved faster. Kathy let out a loud groan of pain and then became silent. He started to panic until he saw how the glow in her eyes disappeared. She closed her eyes and gasped as random parts of her head began glowing.

"Oh crap," Trent said. The knowledge phase. Hang on. This won't last too long."

"What's... happening... to me?"

The entire top of her head glowed briefly before the glow began to fade and her body stopped shaking. She let out a tired sigh before she tried to get up.

"Whoa. Take it easy. Think you should stay down 'til the world stops spinning."

Being as headstrong as she was, she still tried to get up. She got on her hands and knees, and he had to catch her when she tried to get on her feet and almost fell over. He held her tightly in his arms as she leaned against him.

"What was that? I... saw things,... heard things, felt things. I'm starting to..." she said before she rested her head against his shoulder.

"You're slowly starting to understand it all. This is only one phase of your ascent. The knowledge you have now is only a single wave in the ocean of knowledge."

Kathy still looked dizzy and confused when she lifted her head and asked, "Why were there so many of me?"

"You saw all your alternate selves in the alternate physical planes. All the different versions of you that – "

"I saw them all... die. Those two freaks fucking killed all of my... other selves... like animals."

Trent kissed her on her forehead, hugged her, and said, "That's one of the crappy parts of being a planewalker. Seeing versions of yourself being savagely unplugged. I hate to say it but you never really get over that. Only the prime version of a planewalker, the true version of you on the Prime Physical Plane, can ascend when all the alternate versions of you are unplugged."

Kathy let go of him as she began looking at the desert around her. Fearing that she might collapse, Trent didn't want to let go of her at first but she squeezed his forearm and stepped away from him. She kept frowning as she looked at the road and the dunes around her. Even the pile of rocks next to the road looked familiar to her.

"I remember this place. I've never been here before but I remember it. And I remember how my other self... alternate self died here. I was... *she* was killed by what's his name."

"Klouser. I know," he said as he walked up next to her and took her by the hand. "This knowledge phase is scary but its important. There's so much you need to know and understand to be a planewalker."

Kathy still kept looking at the desert as she asked him, "I had a dream... I remember having a dream not so long back where I saw myself running down this road."

"You'll soon realize that every single dream, every nightmare you've ever had was when you and one of your alternate selves connected mentally. Every déjà vu you ever had – "

Trent paused when he saw how Kathy stared at him. She squinted as she stared at his face and moved closer to him.

"You – your face. You're starting to look familiar. I've seen you before."

Trent looked away and said, "That's not important. All that matters now is keeping you safe and you practicing your powers. We have to keep moving to other planes and hope they don't find us, and I have to teach you how to use your powers."

"I can feel these powers in me, but I don't think I can really control any of them yet. Can't you give me a quick lesson, teach me how to use these powers so that we can fight those two and bring this nightmare to an end?"

He stared at her as she walked to the pile of rocks. She wanted to pick up one of the rocks and tell him that they couldn't fight Klouser and Xanthy with rocks, and that they should go to another plane where they could find weapons to use against them. Just as she was about to pick up the rock, the rattlesnake tried to bite her. In that split second that her life was in danger, it felt to her as if everything around her was happening in slow motion. She grabbed the snake with both hands – one hand right behind its head – and bashed its head against one of the big rocks repeatedly until it was dead. Holding the dead snake in one hand, she turned to Trent, smiled, tossed it aside and said, "I might not be at the level you are when it comes to controlling my powers, but I'm getting there. Teach me."

Trent silently whispered to himself, "Cocky as always. That's one of the many reasons I like you."

"I can't hear you. What did you say?"

"I said you only know a fraction of what you need to know and can't control all of your powers yet. You don't know them like I do. They'll do anything to get your powers. If you try to take them on without having full control over your powers, they're going to filet your ass."

He picked up a few small stones on the road and began walking toward her. He looked at the stones in his hand and closed his hand when his palm began to glow.

"Klouser and Xanthy have completely destroyed two alternate physical planes and drained them of their mystical and elemental energies. They want to destroy them all for their energies."

As he walked towards her, Trent opened up his glowing hand. All of the small stones flew out of his hand and struck Kathy against her legs.

"Hey! What are you doing?"

He pointed his glowing hand down at other small stones on the road and used his powers to send them flying towards her. Kathy was struck by a few and managed to dodge the rest.

"Stop that!" she yelled before she grabbed a fist-sized rock off of the ground and threw it at him. The rock was heading straight for his face. It stopped in mid-air and hovered inches in front of his face as he was pointing the glowing palm of his hand up at it.

"You can do better than that," he said.

The rock flew straight back at her and she dodged it just in time. She appeared to be growing more and more annoyed by what he was doing. Using his powers, he made random stones on the road fly up at her from different directions.

"Stop it!" she yelled. Some stones missed her while others struck her on her legs and stomach. When she'd finally had enough with what she considered to be childish games, she pointed her hands down at the road. Her palms glowed as she used her powers to start what looked like a mini whirlwind. A small cloud of whirling sand and small stones formed. The cloud formed a ball of moving air, sand and stones which she sent flying straight at him. Holding up his hand, the ball blew apart before it could reach him.

"Try again!"

Kathy paused as she looked at her glowing hands. She couldn't believe what she'd just done with such little effort. She pointed her hands down at the road again and did the same. When the cloud of air, sand and stone turned into a ball and began flying towards him, she used her powers to make it change form. The ball changed into the shape of a big spearhead. Again, Trent effortlessly blocked her attack.

"That's more like it. You're learning something new about your powers."

Kathy was beyond annoyed. She wanted him to train her, tell her what to do and how to do it, but instead he was turning it into some childish game.

"You're just playing with me?! We don't have time for stupid games!"

Trent smiled at her. Seeing him smile annoyed her even more.

"I had to get you angry," he said. "Your emotional state plays a big role in gaining control over your powers. Anger gets you started. Anger, rage, fear unleashes it. Now you've got to learn to stay calm so you'll have more control over your powers. You've gotten a big taste of your powers, seen what you're capable of doing with your powers. Will you listen to me now?"

"That was a lesson? Teach me more."

Trent pointed at the sand, rocks and road, and said, "There isn't much around here you can use as a weapon. You still attacked me with what little there was to use. Do it again. Attack me."

Kathy looked around and saw the dead snake. She used her powers to make the snake float through the air towards her hand. The snake was still four feet away from her hand when the glow in her hand flickered and the snake fell on the ground.

"Dammit!" she said as she pointed her hand at the snake again.

"You're trying too hard. You're trying to rush it. Remember, calm. Know that you can do it and stay calm."

She took three deep breaths, pointed at the snake and tried again. Blood and venom dripped from the snake's head as it floated up off the ground and hovered in the air. She tilted her head back and tried to clear her mind of all the fears and worries that were distracting her mind. Focusing her mind on her powers, she made the snake fly through the air towards Trent. He used his powers and effortlessly stopped the snake in the air. As he sent it flying back at her, he used his powers to twist the snake into the shape of a heart. She didn't notice this as she used her powers to stop it and sent it flying back to him. This went on for a full minute. They kept trying to attack each other with the snake until he used more of his powers and she couldn't stop it or send it back his way. She had to dodge it. She tried to remain calm like he'd said yet her impatience got the better of her. Kathy tired to use her powers on the sand and stones on the road again. A swirling cloud of sand and stones formed in front of her before she sent it swirling straight at Trent's head. He waved his glowing hand in a circle in front of his face, causing the sand and stones to stop in the air and form a ball before he sent it straight back to her. She tried to stop it but couldn't. It struck her and knocked her off her feet. Trent rushed to Kathy to see if she was hurt.

"Shit. Are you hurt?"

"I'm fine. What was that?" she asked as she got up and dusted herself off. "I tried to stop it but you're much stronger than me. I'm still a rookie with these powers and if those two find us, my lack of control over my powers could get us both killed."

Trent put his hands on her upper arms and told her, "Don't talk like that. Your fears and self-doubts are what hold you back. I know you can gain control over the few powers you have now, and I know in my heart you'll have full control over all your powers when you finish ascending."

She stared into his eyes and tried to remember where she'd seen him before. Staring at him, every little detail on his face looked familiar.

"You've got an awful lot of faith in me for someone who doesn't know me. Are you sure we haven't met before?"

Trent paused like someone who was at a complete loss for words, looked around, looked at her and said, "I... We... I think we better get out of here and move on to another plane. We have to keep moving. You're still too weak to fight them."

As Trent used his powers to open a portal door, Kathy touched his glowing hand. She could feel the energy pulsing through his hand. Another snake emerged from behind a pile of big rocks on the sand as the two leaped into the open portal.

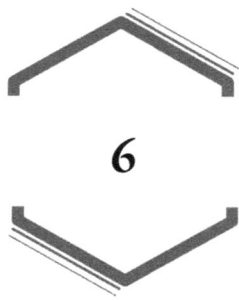

6

In a desert wasteland, between all the dunes, there were still remains of destroyed buildings visible above the surface of the sand. A portal door opened on top of a large dune. Kathy and Trent came leaping out of it and their bodies tumbled head over heels down the side of the dune. When they finally reached the bottom of the dune, both of them were dizzy but neither of them were hurt. Kathy spat out sand that had gotten into her mouth during the tumble. Lying flat on her stomach, it still felt to her as if the world was spinning. She could feel the pain and burning sensations in her body but it wasn't as bad as it had been before. When her dizziness finally started to fade away, the first thing she noticed was the human skull partially visible above the surface of the sand. Trent got up and began looking around as he asked her if she was hurt. Kathy got on her hands and knees, and felt the pain and burning sensations moving in waves up and down her entire body.

"Is the pain starting to fade?" Trent asked.

"You said it gets better after a few trips through the Transition Plane. It's not as bad as it was before but it still hurts like a bitch."

The blue glow was still flickering in her eyes as he helped her up. Still dizzy, she held on to his arm as they looked around at the destruction. Once her dizziness had faded, they made their way up one of the dunes and looked at what little there was left to see in the wasteland.

"What plane is this?" she asked.

Trent breathed out a long guilt-filled sigh before he replied, "I remember this plane. Or at least, I remember what it was. This used to be an alternative physical plane."

"What happened here? Looks like there was a war."

"It wasn't a war. It was the lust for more power that did this," Trent said. He clenched his fists, looked at Kathy, and said, "After getting most of the powers he has now, Klouser wanted more powers. He didn't just want to kill all the planewalkers on this plane. He wanted to kill everyone and everything on this plane so that he could drain the entire plane of its mystical and elemental powers. He wanted every form of energy he could take from this plane."

Kathy shook her head in disbelief. She was starting to realize how much power a planewalker actually had and how that power could corrupt one into doing the unthinkable just to gain more powers. She looked around at all the destruction around her and it all seemed so unreal.

"No way," she said. "Impossible. One man – or, one planewalker – could do all this damage. Is he really that powerful to do all this?"

"Not just Klouser. Xanthy... and I helped him kill all the planewalkers, people, and everything else on this plane." He pointed at all the destruction as far as the eye could see. "Most of what you see, we helped him to drain the powers from living beings and to destroy things, but he did a lot of the destroying on his own as he gained more powers. If he kills the two of us and takes our powers, he'll be able to do things far worse than this."

"Your powers too?" Kathy asked, sounding confused. "I thought you said he only wants my powers."

"He needs the powers of at least two more planewalkers to reach the level of powers he wants. There might still be a few other planewalkers out there that we don't know about, but I highly doubt it. We killed so many. I believe we are the only four that are left. I don't care what happens to me. If they find us and they kill me and take my powers, I don't care. As long as they don't get you, and as long as I can protect you 'til you finish ascending and gain full control over your powers."

Kathy put her arm around his waist and looked at his face. He tried his hardest to keep a straight face as he spoke to her but she could tell that he was feeling guilty for everything he'd done while he was working for Klouser and Xanthy. She found it strange that she could tell all this by just looking at him and listening to him. She felt that she could read his expressions and emotions like a book, as if she'd known him for years.

"If they need the powers of two more planewalkers, why didn't you just save yourself? That would've stopped Klouser from getting all the powers he wants. Right?"

As simple a question as this was, Trent didn't want to answer her. He took her by the hand and began leading her down the other side of the dune.

"If Klouser reaches that level of power, he would be able to do more than just move between planes and have immense telekinetic powers. He'd be able to enter and move freely in the Transition Plane."

"You mean he'd be able to fight those spirits?"

"The Guardians? Yes. He'd be able to defeat them and take over the Transition Plane."

Trent could tell by the look on Kathy's face that she didn't have a clue what Klouser would be able to do if he took over the Transition Plane. At the bottom of the dune, between all the remains of buildings, cars and an airplane, Trent picked up a human skull. He held it in front of Kathy, mere inches from her face. She turned her head to look away.

"Look at this."

She hesitantly looked at the skull.

"This is only one of the billions of lives Klouser took in his never-ending quest for more power. If he gains our powers, he'd be able to do much worse. I remember from the time I... I was their follower, he and Xanthy talked about how they wanted enough power to take control of the Transition Plane and to merge all of the planes – except Heaven, of course."

"Heaven?"

He tossed the skull over his shoulder, and replied, "Yes, Heaven. It's much more than a plane. Do you know what will happen if they merge all the other planes? They will form one plane of physical and spiritual chaos. People, lost souls, demons, monsters that some writer with a twisted imagination thought up, you name it, all of them will be together on one plane that will be ruled by Klouser and Xanthy."

Kathy took another look at the devastation and destruction around her. She hid her fear well when she looked at Trent, and said, "If the three of you could do all this damage with your powers, how much damage could I do to them when I learn to control all of my powers? Teach me. Help me to gain control over my powers."

"I can only teach you so much before you finish ascending," he said before he took one of his gutter blades in its sheath off of his belt and handed it to her. "What we can do to prepare you, in case they find us, is to get you familiar with this."

She pulled the blade from its sheath and looked at its strange shape. Trent stepped back and said, "Don't go swinging that thing around all willy-nilly. You could accidentally slice off your nose, or you could slice off something of mine and force me to change my name to Tina."

She smiled at his sarcasm as she put the blade back in its sheath. Trent could tell by the way she looked at her new weapon that she was eager to learn how to fight with it.

"Put that on your belt and get ready. We have to leave this plane. We've got to keep moving."

Having the gutter blade in its sheath on her belt felt strange. She took him by the hand as he opened a portal door and they leaped into it.

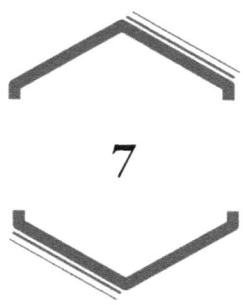

7

On another alternate physical plane, Klouser and Xanthy were continuing their search for Kathy and Trent. They'd been searching for more than an hour around the area where the portal door had opened. Both of them were growing impatient and frustrated. Of all the people they saw out on the street, they almost attacked a young couple who, from behind, looked a lot like Kathy and Trent. They were walking through an alley when Klouser saw a vagrant sleeping under a dirty blanket on top of large pieces of cardboard. His palms began to glow as he walked towards the vagrant.

"What are you doing? We have to keep hunting for those two," Xanthy said.

Klouser crouched down next to the vagrant and pressed his palms against the vagrant's chest. The poor vagrant woke up but there was nothing he could do to stop him. He didn't even have enough energy left in his body to fight back or to scream as all of his energy was being sucked out of his body. His entire body turned pitch black and his skin cracked open. Smoke rose out of the dead vagrant's body as Klouser walked away from him and angrily swung his fist through the air.

"So little power. These normal humans don't have enough energy in them to make me more powerful."

"Hey, every little bit helps. You know how powerful you are already. Without my help, it wouldn't take you too long to kill everyone and destroy everything on this plane, and drain every living thing of its energy," Xanthy said.

Klouser touched a trashcan with his glowing thumb. The entire trashcan was sent flying down the alley. As it traveled through the air, some parts of it and the garbage in it burnt into ashes and other parts of it turned to dust. Xanthy groped his butt and stroked his ego by complementing him for how powerful he was.

"It's not enough! I need their powers. If there were other planewalkers somewhere out there, we could hunt them down and take their powers, but as far as we know there aren't any others. I hope the drones are having more luck. Maybe if the drones find them and fight them, they could at least injure them and keep them busy fighting long enough for us to find them."

"We'll find them. And when we do so, we can finally unplug them both and give you all the powers that you deserve. When we merge all the planes, you'll rule the new world with me by your side."

She kissed Klouser and they continued on their way down the alley. They climbed up the fire escape of an apartment building. When they reached the roof, they stared down at the people in the street. Their eyes glowed as they pointed their hands down at the people. Using their powers and planewalker senses, they were trying to sense if there was anyone there with planewalker powers. After doing this for short while, Klouser opened a portal door and the two moved on to the next plane to continue their hunt.

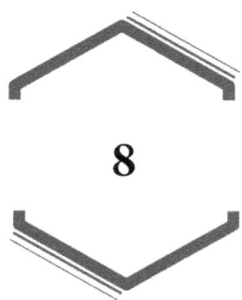

8

On the roof of an office building, Kathy and Trent were busy doing some much needed fight training. In stead of asking him to train her how to fight with her gutter blade, she'd pulled out her blade and attacked him with it – forcing him to train her right there and then. Sparks flew through the air every time their blades met. During the first seven minutes of the training, she could tell that he was holding back.

"Come on! What are you waiting for? Fight me like you'd fight a stronger planewalker!" she yelled.

He knew she needed all the fight training she could get, but there was a reason he was holding back. She kept blocking his blade as his attack began forcing her backwards towards the edge of the roof. She tried to attack him but he blocked her blade with his, grabbed her by the arm, twisted it, kicked her leg out from under her and pressed his blade against the back of her neck.

"And you're unplugged. I could've unplugged you a dozen times by now! Get up! Again!"

Kathy got up and didn't wait for him to step back before she attacked him. He could tell that she was fighting him with a clouded mind. Fear, anger, and frustration were making her fight like a mad woman.

"Calm your mind!" he yelled as he blocked her attacks. "Trust me! Keep fighting, but just calm your mind!"

She tried to do what he was saying. She tried to block out all the fear she had of being found by Klouser and Xanthy, and she tried to block out all the anger and frustration she felt for not having full control over her powers yet. Her first attempts to calm her mind failed. She was attacking him more aggressively. He fought back and knocked the blade out of her hand. He leaned closer to her as he pressed the tip of his blade against her collarbone, and said, "This isn't the Kathy I know. You're a fighter. You're strong. And deep inside of you, you know how to control your mind and you know how to fight like a pro. Just remember it! Again!"

Kathy picked up her blade as he took two steps back. She attacked him before he even had a chance to raise his blade. Luckily, he dodged her blade and they continued fighting. Kathy didn't expect what he was going to do next. She saw how his eyes began glowing bright blue. All of a sudden, it didn't feel like fight training anymore. He was attacking her so aggressively that for a moment she began fearing for her life. Instead of allowing her fears and self-doubt to cloud her mind, she did what he'd told her to do: she stayed calm and fought back. She didn't notice it but her eyes also began glowing as she fought faster. At first, Trent managed to block every one of her attacks. The glow in her eyes grew brighter as she fought faster and began forcing him backwards towards the edge of the roof. Her legs started to feel like jelly and she was starting to feel dizzy. What was happening to her?! She forced herself to stay calm and continued fighting until she became so dizzy that she dropped her blade. She dropped down on her knees and a glowing spot appeared in the middle of her forehead.

"What's happening to me?"

Trent smiled as he crouched down next to her and put his hand on her shoulder.

"You know how to fight and how to use your powers. All you have to do is remember. All the powers and knowledge of all your alternate selves are inside of you. As you ascend, you gain their powers. And as your mind's eye is slowly opened, you start remembering everything that's trapped and hidden inside your own mind. Among all the knowledge still trapped in your mind is the knowledge of fighting with a gutter blade," he said before he got up, picked up her blade, handed it to her, and whispered with a smile, "Again."

She took her blade from him and got back on her feet. The dizziness was starting to fade. At first he kept his blade raised, waiting for her to attack him. Then he lowered his blade. By doing this, he was basically asking her to attack him. Kathy grinned as she raised her blade and attacked him. For more than ten minutes, both of them were fighting each other as if their lives depended on it. Her eyes kept glowing and the veins in her face and neck also briefly glowed bright blue. Out of breath from their intense fight training, he said, "You're... getting better... Rosebud."

At the very moment he said her nickname, she looked at his face. The glow in her eyes grew brighter and spread up into her forehead. She tried not to drop her blade and to continue fighting, but the dizziness came back and she began seeing images in her mind.

"Your face – " was all she said as her blade fell out of her hand.

"Wow. You're ascending fast. Just let in all the powers and knowledge and it'll – "

"I remember your face. I know I've seen you before. I remember you holding my hand. We were inside a cave. And I remember you and I running away from something. We were running between a bunch of cars in a parking lot. What aren't you telling me?"

Trent paused. He appeared to be too afraid to answer her.

"I don't think you're ready to hear this," he said.

"Don't feed me that crap! I remember you from somewhere. I remember being with you. What are you hiding from me? Give me the truth."

"I don't think you're ready for this truth. The thing about some truths are that they hurt. All we should focus on now is keeping you safe, moving from plane to plane, and to keep training so that you can finish ascending."

"You want to train me and get me used to my powers while I'm still ascending. I get that and I appreciate that, but a little more truth would help me a hell of a lot right now."

"You'll remember more as you ascend. You and I both will know when you'll be ready to hear the truth. Let's get going."

She stared angrily at him as he opened a portal door. He held out his hand to her. She shook her head and breathed out an angry sigh before she took him by the hand and they leaped into the open portal door. If he was really there to protect her and to help her while she was ascending, what possible reason would he have to be keeping secrets from her?

CHAPTER III

1

In what appeared to be a poor urban area, the streets and alleyways were dirty. Besides how dirty and run-down everything appeared, there was something else that was strange. There were cars parked in many of the parking spots all along the streets, but there wasn't a single car driving up or down any of the streets. There were many people wandering around. Some wandered into buildings, some wandered in circles in the streets, and others were talking to themselves as they wandered up or down the sidewalk. Who were these people?

A portal door opened in front of a retail store close to the corner of the street. Kathy and Trent came leaping out through the portal door. They stumbled across the sidewalk and fell to their hands and knees in an empty parking spot. Kathy was the first of the two to get up. She could still feel burning sensations in certain areas of her body but clearly – thanks to her powers – her body was becoming used to moving through the Transition Plane. She began looking around at all the people wandering around them. The first thought in her mind was that this was a plane for people who were insane. To her, every single person she saw wandering around looked crazy. Trent got up, looked around and shook his head.

"Shit. I haven't been on this plane in ages. This plane still creeps me out. They are way more now than they were the last time that I was here," he said.

"What's wrong with all of them? They all look like they're a bit nuts in the head. Where are we?"

An elderly woman was walking towards Trent. Kathy thought the woman wanted to ask them something. Imagine her shock when the woman walked straight through Trent. He couldn't stop himself from grinning when he saw the shocked look on Kathy's face.

"This plane is Limbo," he said.

"Wait a minute. So you mean all of these people..."

"Yup. All of these people are dead. Sad thing is, none of these poor bastards know that they're dead. They're wandering souls."

Kathy kept looking around at all the souls as she slowly walked to the middle of the street. Everyone she looked at had the same frightened, confused expression on their face. Trent joined her in the middle of the street.

"But how?" she asked. "You spoke about Heaven earlier. Why aren't their souls in Heaven?"

"It's one thing to die and to go upstairs if you were good, or downstairs if you were bad. Going to the other side isn't always that simple. Each one of these souls can't find peace, can't accept that they're dead because they had so much good they still wanted to do on the planes of the living, or they can't let go of all their loved ones they're leaving behind. Some of them that – I think – are going to end up downstairs don't want to move on thanks to all the hate in their souls, all the grudges they carried throughout their lives. It's like a war inside them that keeps them from accepting their fate."

Trent told her more about the plane they were on as they walked up the street. Kathy couldn't stop looking at the wandering souls as they walked. When she finally stopped staring at them, she stared at Trent while listening to him talking about how he'd tried in vain in the past to talk to the souls.

"I tried everything I could think of to communicate with the wandering souls, and to tell them that it would be better if they moved on to their final destination. I felt like a dumbass because none of them could hear me or see me. I still tried to – "

"I remember you from my dreams," she interrupted him. She took a step back, pointed at him, nodded her head, and said, "Yes. I knew it. I knew when I saw you that I've seen you before. You were in a few of my dreams."

Clearly this was an awkward moment. They stood there speechless for almost a minute just staring at each other. Three wandering souls walked straight through both of them as Trent tried to think of a way to explain why she'd seen him in her dreams, and she stood there impatiently waiting for an answer that she felt she was owed.

"You told me that dreams happen when anybody connects with one of their alternate selves on an alternate physical plane. If that's right, then it means – "

Trent lowered his head and raised his hand to silence her. Seeing the look on his face made it clear to her that her question had struck an emotional nerve. She could tell that he was feeling sad and was trying his hardest not to show it.

"You want the truth, the whole truth of why you remember me," he said. "When I was working with Klouser and Xanthy... When I was still one of the bad guys hunting down other planewalkers and their alternate selves to unplug them for their powers, I felt I was like a hitman with a mission. Every – " he paused and looked around at the wandering souls, hoping Kathy didn't see the tears in his eyes, and the shame and regret he felt. "Every time I killed someone, I felt I was doing it for a greater cause. Those two had me convince that, with all the powers Xanthy and I had gained, we were better than any other planewalker or any other normal human. They had me convince that if Klouser gained all the powers he needed to have enough powers and control over his powers to take over the Transition Plane, we would be changing the whole world. They had me thinking that with all the bad we were doing, it would all be to change all the planes in the world for a good reason."

Trent shook his head in shame as he walked to the nearest car and leaned against it. Kathy walked up to him and held out her hand. He took her by the hand, and continued, "I was an idiot. A killer who thought I was killing for a good reason, but deep down I knew they were bad news. I knew they were evil. We kept hunting planewalkers and their alternate selves until we thought there was only one left. There could still be many more out there we don't know about but we thought you were the last one left. We... we began killing your alternate selves."

Kathy pulled her hand out of his, took a step back and shook her head as she asked, "You mean, you helped them to kill all my alternate selves?!"

Shocked by what he was confessing to her, she wanted to turn around and walk away from him.

"There was one of your alternate selves I couldn't unplug."

Looking at him as he stared down at the ground, she could see the tears dripping from his eyes. She could feel his warm breath on her cold hand as she touched his face, put her hand underneath his chin and lifted his head to look him in the eyes. Seeing his face as he showed these emotions unlocked another memory. She remembered what he and one of her alternate selves did together.

"You... I remember you with me," she paused as she tried to find the right words to say it. "I remember you making love to me."

"I fell in love with you! Okay. Or, at least, I fell in love with one of your alternate selves. And it was thanks to that that I couldn't keep killing like some heartless monster."

She leaned closer and hugged him. Feeling his arms around her awakened memories and feelings in her heart and mind. She gained more memories from her last alternate self that Trent had had a secret relationship with. Besides remembering in vivid detail how passionately they made love, she remembered how he did everything he could to protect her from Klouser and Xanthy.

"What can I say? Just because I'm a planewalker doesn't mean that my heart isn't human. I have feelings and emotions like everyone else," Trent said while he pretended to wipe sweat from his forehead and wiped the tears from his eyes and cheeks.

"What happened? What made you turn against them?"

"I was an idiot in the beginning when they made me part of their sick plan to kill all the other planewalkers. They had me thinking that all the bad we were doing was for a good reason. I was a fucking killing machine until we began hunting down and unplugging your alternate selves. We were hunting for one version of you in the city. She was hiding somewhere in a apartment building. The three of us split up and looked for her on every floor of the building. I found her hiding in a janitor's closet on the sixth floor. She grabbed a broom and wanted to fight me with it. I had my blade in my hand, ready to unplug her, then I looked into her eyes and something inside me just screamed *'WRONG!!!'*. She pushed me out of the way and tried to run but I grabbed her. She put up a fight 'til I put my blade away and told her to stop fighting me and to trust me..."

Kathy saw tears streaming down his face as he chuckled and said, "Then she kicked me in the balls, punched me and ran. I went after her. She wanted to make a run for it down the stairs but saw Klouser with his blade coming up the stairs. I followed her up the stairs to the tenth floor where I grabbed her, and forced her into the elevator. We got out of the building and made a run for it, hoping Klouser and Xanthy would never find us."

Four wandering souls walked towards Trent with curious expressions on their faces. They could sense his sadness and heartbreak, and even though they couldn't see him, this drew them towards him. Kathy and Trent walked away from them and went into one of the shops across the street. There, Trent continued to tell her how he and her alternate self were on the run for what felt like ages. During this time, they started falling in love with each other. He told her how they used to spend nights in abandoned buildings, empty apartments, warehouses, etc. They kept moving from one random place to the next hoping they would never be found.

"We traveled all over the place, thinking we would be safe if we kept moving to random places. They almost caught us four times but we kept running, hoping they might give up after a while. And then they found us..."

He continued to describe to Kathy in detail what happened when Klouser and Xanthy found him and her alternate self:

On the outskirts of a small town, there was an abandoned old farm. Trent and Kathy's alternate self had been hiding out there for only two days and were preparing to leave. They were in the kitchen busy putting a few fruits they'd picked, from the different trees growing next to the barn, into a bag when Klouser and Xanthy entered the farmhouse. They grabbed their belongings and ran out the backdoor.

Outside, they ran towards the barn. Trent pointed his hand out in front of him and was starting to open a portal door when Klouser and Xanthy came running out through the backdoor. The portal door opened. Xanthy pointed her hand at a pitchfork that was among other old rusty tools in a big pile on the ground. She used her telekinetic powers to make the pitchfork fly though the air like a spear. Just as Trent and that alternate version of Kathy were about to jump into the open portal door hand in hand, the pitchfork struck her in her lower back. She screamed as her hand slipped out of his and she fell to the ground. Trent screamed out her name as he was being sucked into the open portal door. They killed her. The feeling of helplessness was overwhelming. As he was frozen in the air in the Transition Plane, he could do nothing to save her. Knowing how heartless those two were, he knew she was dead. He was actually lucky not to have witnessed how brutally Klouser and Xanthy tortured her before they killed her. After that tragic incident, Trent began his search for Kathy on the Prime Physical Plane. He, who'd once been an obedient slave and a heartless killing machine for Klouser and Xanthy, was changed by this tragedy. Love, loss, sorrow and rage had awoken the warrior in him, and that was why he would do whatever it took to protect and prepare the last remaining version of Kathy on the Prime Physical Plane.

Listening to Trent sharing such a horrific memory made Kathy understand why he was so protective of her. Even as he spoke, some of what he said made her remember more of her dreams she'd seen him in. When she touched his face to wipe the tears from his cheek, more memories flooded through her mind, but these weren't dreams. She saw more than two dozen memories – playing through her mind like video clips – of times her alternate self and Trent spent together while they were on the run.

"That's why I rebelled against them, and that's why we need to keep you safe and get you ready to fight with your blade and your powers. We can't run forever," he said.

She looked around and saw the door at the back of the shop. Trent followed her as she walked to the door, opened it and looked outside. The alley behind the shop was empty. No souls were wandering around in it.

"Looking for something?" he asked.

She stepped outside, pulled out her blade and said, "This is a good place to do more training."

Trent smiled as he stepped out of the shop, pulled out his blade and attacked her. The souls wandering past the entrance to the alley didn't distract them as they fought.

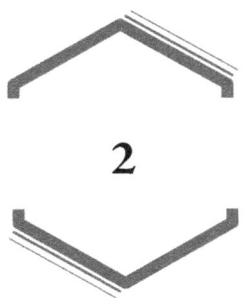

2

On an alternate physical plane, Klouser and Xanthy looked like two psychos on a mission as they continued their hunt. It was raining heavily. They were searching through an old abandoned building close to the edge of the city where a few vagrants lived. They searched through the entire building. Every vagrant that saw them ran away. Klouser became so frustrated that he wanted to kill a vagrant just to relieve his frustration. Xanthy stopped him when she saw him pulling out his blade.

"Don't waste your energy and time on a human. The more time we waste, the longer it's going to take us to find them," she said.

He agreed with her and they left the building. They searched between the small houses in a low cost housing project close to the abandoned building before he opened a portal door and they moved on to the next plane.

3

In the alley, Kathy and Trent were still busy with fight training. Her eyes kept glowing and her fighting skills kept improving. He didn't want to make her overconfident by telling her how impressed he was. Besides getting much better with her blade, she began using some of her other powers as well while they fought. As their blades clashed and she drove him back towards the alley's entrance, she used her telekinetic powers to rip a shop's backdoor clean off of its hinges and sent it flying straight at him. Trent ran out of the alley and took cover around the corner just in time. The door flew through the air and struck a car on the other side of the street. Kathy knew she shouldn't get cocky with her powers but she couldn't stop herself from smiling as she came running out of the alley. They continued fighting. Both were so focused on the fight that neither of them allowed the wandering souls to distract them. She drove him back until he bumped into a parked car. He used his telekinetic powers to rip the car's passenger door off and sent it flying straight at her. She dodged it and used her powers to rip the rear door off of the same car and sent it flying at him. He ran and took cover between two parked cars. Shards of a shattered windshield rained down on him as the door struck the car on his left and tore half of its roof off. Both of them smiled as he came out from between the cars and they continued fighting.

Unbeknownst to them, a portal door was opening in the alley. Klouser and Xanthy came leaping out of it. Just as she was about to ask him where they should search first, both of them heard the sounds of blades clashing. Both pulled out their gutter blades and ran down the alley. When they reached the street, they saw Kathy and Trent fighting. Klouser pointed his glowing hand at them and stomped his foot. The ground shook. The windows of shops and cars shattered. Kathy and Trent's hearts and minds filled with fear when they saw them. He grabbed her by her hand and yelled, "Quick! Run!"

She pulled her hand free, turned to face Klouser and Xanthy, and raised her gutter blade.

"What the fuck are you doing?!" Trent yelled.

Klouser and Xanthy laughed at Kathy before they raised their blades and began running towards her. Trent pointed his glowing hand down at all the shards from the shattered windshield and made them all fly through the air like glass bullets. The shards struck them and tore into their chests, stomachs and arms, but they kept running. Klouser swung his blade at her face. She blocked it, stumbled a step back and attacked him. Their blades began clashing and when she slashed him across his hand, Xanthy tried to attack her from the side. Trent attacked her and the two began a hate-filled sword fight. The animosity they felt towards each other couldn't be described in words. As he fought her, he also took a few swings at Klouser, and he kept yelling at Kathy to run. To anyone who didn't have a clue who they were, what they were, or what was going on, this fight would have looked like crazy fight between four mad lunatics. Oblivious to the fighting taking place on their plane, the wandering souls kept wandering straight through all four of them. Kathy thought she had enough control over her powers and enough fighting skills to take on Klouser. She was starting to regret her decision. As hard as she tried to fight him off and to injure him bad enough so that she could unplug him, he was simply too strong. He'd slashed her numerous times already and almost managed to stab his blade into her chest twice. She was losing this fight.

Xanthy used her powers to block Trent's blade and slashed him across his chest. When she tried to do it a second time, he used his powers send her entire body flying though the air. She screamed before her body struck a car. Trent kept yelling at Kathy to run as he attacked Klouser. His words fell on deaf ears. She was injured and bleeding from all her cuts but she refused to run. She cut Klouser across his stomach when he blocked Trent's blade. She was about to stab him in his chest when he punched her in the face and used his powers to send her body tumbling backwards like a rag doll. Trent attacked him and fought like Klouser had never witnessed before. All the love, heartbreak, and rage he had in his heart combined to unleash a fury within him that made him fight better than he'd ever fought before. Klouser managed to cut him four times yet he kept attacking. When he tried to use his powers to kill him, Trent slashed him across his throat, punched him in the face and stabbed him twice in his chest.

"Nooo!!!" Xanthy screamed as she ran towards him. Klouser fell to his knees as Xanthy and Trent began fighting. Instead of using their blades, they used their powers on each other. Dazed, Kathy grabbed her blade and was busy getting up when she saw Klouser on his knees, bleeding profusely and glowing as his wounds started to heal. When she saw how Trent and Xanthy were fighting, she fought through her dizziness, got up and ran to help him. Both of their bodies kept moving through the air and slamming into things as they used their powers on each other. Xanthy's body slammed against the wall of one of the shops. Trent was slammed down on the side walk when Kathy reached him and used her powers to send Xanthy flying into a shop through a window. She helped Trent up and the they began running away. Klouser's wounds were still healing when he got back on his feet and began running after them. Seconds later, Xanthy came running out of the shop and joined the chase. When they reached the corner of the street, Trent was about to open a portal door when a stop sign came flying through the air and struck him down from behind. He used his powers to send the stop sign straight back at them. Klouser dodged it and Xanthy cut it in half with one swing of her blade.

"That the best you can do?! Pathetic!" Xanthy yelled.

As he got up, Trent used his powers to make all four doors fly off of a parked car. Kathy pointed her hands at the doors. Just as Klouser and Xanthy were about to dodge the first two doors, and use their powers to send the other two doors straight back at Trent, Kathy used her powers to do the unexpected. Hurt and bleeding, she used her powers to break the doors apart into small pieces. The pieces that they couldn't dodge or deflect away from themselves with their powers struck them and tore through their flesh. At the very moment that their bodies struck the sidewalk, their bleeding wounds began glowing as they started to heal. Trent did something foolish. He knew his number one mission was to protect and train Kathy. Seeing Klouser and Xanthy hurt and bleeding seemed like a perfect opportunity to kill them both and insure Kathy's safety. Clearly he'd forgotten just how powerful Klouser was. Kathy had her blade in hand as she followed Trent. Klouser saw them running towards him with their blades in hand. He let out a loud angry shout as he fought through the pain and used his power. A streetlight next to him glowed as it broke in half and the top half flew straight at Kathy and Trent. It struck them with such force that it carried them through the air for at least thirty meters before their bodies fell to the ground. The pain both felt all over their bodies was indescribable. Side by side on their backs on the sidewalk, Trent's face was covered in blood from the cuts on his forehead. Hurt and disorientated, he tried to get up as he kept repeating, "We have to go! Come on!"

As hurt as Kathy was, she didn't even notice how bright her bleeding wounds were glowing as they started to heal. She yelled at him to get up as she got up and saw Klouser and Xanthy getting back on their feet. She was busy helping Trent up when she saw Klouser and Xanthy doing something strange. He was pointing his hands down at the sidewalk as he walked and she was walking right behind him with both glowing hands on his shoulders. When Trent saw this, Kathy could see the expression of fear on his blood covered face. He grabbed her by the arm and yelled at the top of his lungs, "MOVE!!!"

She stumbled as he pushed her through the open door of the nearest shop. Streams of dim blue light came out of virtually everything in front of Klouser as he drained everything in sight of its energy. Everything in his path was destroyed. The sidewalks, the street, the cars, the street signs, and the fronts of all the shops and stores were torn apart. Most of everything that was being drained of its energy was destroyed and turned into nothing more than a mixture of sand and dust. The bits and pieces that weren't being turned into sand and dust flew all over the place. The deafening noise outside was unbearable as Kathy and Trent made their way through the cluttered shop to the backdoor. The ground was shaking and the sand and dust that blew into the shop forced them to hold their breaths until they reached the backdoor and ran out into the alley. Trent grabbed her by the hand, opened a portal door and they escaped. As the portal door closed and disappeared, Klouser and Xanthy were still busy destroying everything in their sight and draining everything of energy. After a full two minutes of doing this, he finally lowered his hands and stopped. He was angry and frustrated that they didn't catch, unplug and drain Kathy and Trent of their powers, but seeing the destruction he'd caused and feeling what little energy he'd drained from everything in front of him boosted his ego a little.

"They can't have gotten far," Xanthy said. "If we hurry we could still catch them."

Klouser grabbed her by the hand as she walked past him, and said, "They're already gone. I doubt that either of them are foolish enough to try and outrun us after seeing how powerful I have become."

Klouser looked down at all the glowing spots on his body as his wounds continued to heal on their own. He took Xanthy by the hand, opened a portal door, and they continued their hunt for Kathy and Trent.

After the portal door closed and disappeared, the wandering souls continued wandering up and down the sand in the stretch that had been destroyed, totally oblivious to what had just happened on their plane.

4

A portal door opened inside a pitch black cave. Kathy and Trent came leaping out of it. Falling on the cold wet floor of the cave only added to their injuries. Neither of them had the chance to look around to see where they were before the portal door closed and disappeared. The faint glow from their healing wounds didn't provide enough light for them to see much around them.

"Tre- Trent..." she whispered.

Still holding hands, he squeezed her hand to let her know he was still alive. He opened his mouth to say something and only managed to breath out a loud sigh. He had five broken ribs and just breathing was indescribably painful. The extent of her injuries was also severe. Both remained silent and just squeezed each other's hands every now and then as their wounds healed. Feeling the tears tickling his face as they streamed from his eyes provided little comfort to him as he felt the pain of each of his broken ribs as they healed. Kathy felt the same pain as her three broken ribs healed and the blood went back into each of her bleeding organs. After the minutes that felt like hours finally passed and their injuries were completely healed, they got up. Not knowing where they were, both were too scared to speak. They remained dead silent as he used one hand to hold her by the wrist, and made his other hand glow to light the way as they began looking for the cave's exit.

They finally saw a dim glowing red light ahead and made their way to the cave's exit. The red glow grew brighter and brighter the closer they came to the exit. When they stepped out of the cave, she almost fell down the enormous pit in front of the cave. Trent pulled her back and used his other hand to cover his mouth and nose. Kathy immediately felt sick to her stomach when she also smelled the disgusting stench in the air. Before covering her mouth and nose, she asked, "What the fuck is that? Raw sewage? Where are we?"

"I remember this rotting stench. We're in – "

"Helllloooo Trent," Lucifer said.

Kathy looked across the pit and saw the Devil sitting on his stone throne. He had scars all over his bald head. His once snow white robe was torn and stained pitch black. His feet were shackled and chained to his throne. He spread the shredded and burnt remains of his angel wings as he stood up, pointed at Trent and said, "This is my world! You can't come and go here whenever you please!"

The sound of a faint scream in the distance drew Kathy's attention. She looked up and saw the soul of a dead corrupt politician falling. She could hear the terror in the soul's scream as it fell past where she stood. When she looked down, she saw the lake of fire at the bottom of the pit where the souls of the damned burned for their sins. Luckily, it was too far down for her to see much of what was going on down there. If she had seen all the pain, torture and suffering in the lake of fire, it would've drove her insane.

Lucifer breathed out a satisfied sigh and said, "And another one bites the brimstone."

Trent pulled Kathy away from the edge of the pit, back into the dark cave. Lucifer began screaming Trent's name and yelled, "You'll be back! You'll end up here for good one day! You hear me!"

Trent stepped out of the cave, smiled, winked at him and flipped him the finger before he went back into the cave. He and Kathy made their way back to where the portal door had opened. Kathy was shocked by what she'd just seen. She didn't say a word as she held Trent by the hand and he opened the portal door.

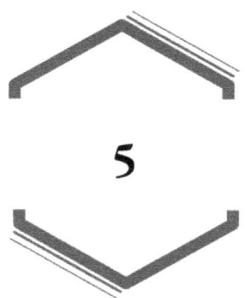

5

A portal door opened in what appeared to be an old abandoned playground. Kathy and Trent came out through it and fell on the grass. Before she could get up, he began arguing with her.

"What were you thinking back there? Did you really think you could take on Klouser and Xanthy on your own?"

"In case you forgot, we saved each other's asses. I might not know how to control all of my powers yet, but I think I know enough to take on those two."

Trent sighed, shook his head, and said, "You know how to use some, maybe even most of your powers. That's what makes all of us get cocky. As soon as you get a taste of your powers, you think that you're indestructible. But you're not! And, yes, thanks for saving my ass. Just know that being cocky with your powers is just as bad as being too afraid to use them. It'll get you killed."

He kept looking around as he helped her up. After their fight with Klouser and Xanthy, he knew that the chances of the four of them ending up on the same plane wasn't as slim as he'd thought. He kissed her on her forehead, and said, "I've seen too many versions of you die. I'm not gonna let that happen again."

"I guess I was kinda on a power trip," she said.

"The powers do that to all of us in the beginning. You think you can fight and control your powers. Show me what you got."

Kathy looked around and saw a sandbox between the swings and the see-saw. She walked up to the sandbox and pointed her hand at the sand in it. The sand began moving as her palm started to glow. The sand began swirling up towards her hand. She was controlling the sand and made it swirl in a big spiral around her hand. Trent shook his head as he walked towards her.

"No, no, no," he said. "Learning to control your powers requires more than just playing with dirt. Show me what you can do."

The swirling sand fell back into the sandbox when she turned to face him, and said, "I controlled more of my powers while we were fighting them. You saw what I did."

"Sure, if you're in the middle of a life-threatening situation, you might tap into more of your powers and have control over them while you know you're in danger. You're not in danger now, so show me what you can do."

Kathy looked around and pointed her hand at a tree a short distance behind him. A piece of a branch broke off, flew through the air and hit him against the back of his head.

"Ouch! Hey!... Again! Attack me with something else. You can do better than that."

She pointed her hand at a pile of dead leaves under another tree. The entire pile began to move towards him. Before she could use her powers to turn the leaves into a weapon to attack him with, he faked a loud yawn, pointed his hand at the moving pile, snapped his fingers and blew it up into the air. Dead leaves were raining down on both of them as he turned to face her, and said, "Do you want to attack me or not? Leaves? What would you attack me with if I was Klouser or Xanthy? Imagine you're back there in Limbo. I'm Klouser and Xanthy running down the sidewalk straight at you. What do you do?! Again!"

Instead of giving her the chance to look around for something she could manipulate and control with her powers, he surprised her with an attack. He pointed his hand at the swings. One of the swings came flying through the air with its rusty chains spinning. She used her powers to rip the see-saw out of the ground and it flew in front of the swing. It's chains wrapped around the see-saw. Trent had to run out of the way and the see-saw missed him by a few inches before it plowed into the ground.

"That's better! Again!" he yelled.

Kathy walked straight towards him, pointing her hands at him, using her powers to push him back. With his feet skidding across the ground, he looked at her, tilted his head to the side and faked another yawn to tell her she could do better than that. She used more of her powers and made him stumble backwards.

"Oh, I'm so scared," he said in a sarcastic, mocking tone. "You can do much more than this! Attack me!"

She pointed at what remained of the swings, made it break apart into pieces and sent them flying through the air straight at him. He dodged most of the pieces and used his powers to deflect the rest.

"Dodge this!" she yelled.

She pointed at the jungle gym a short distance behind him. The entire thing broke apart and the metal bars came flying through the air straight at him. He dodged the first few and used his powers to make the other bars fly straight into each other and twist together. The ball of twisted metal bars fell on the ground right next to him. He was about to tell her to try harder when she surprised him with another attack. She used her powers to make the two chains that were wrapped around the see-saw fly off of it. Before he could use his powers to block her attack, both chains began wrapping around his body. He fell to the ground and felt how the chains were tightening around him to the point that he couldn't breathe.

"Okay... You're... getting better," he said before he used his powers to break the chains.

Kathy kept her hands up as he got up. Looking at her, he could tell that she was prepared for a fight. He walked up to her and took her by the hand.

"What? The training is over?" she asked, sounding disappointed.

"The rush of using your powers in a fight never gets old. Let's get cleaned up and then we can continue the training."

There was a gas station across the street from the playground. They went to the restroom and washed the blood from their faces and their healed wounds. He could tell by her eagerness to learn more that she was still feeling the rush. He took her back to the playground, opened a portal door and they moved on to the next plane.

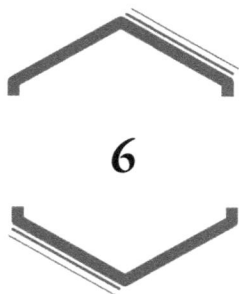

6

On another alternate physical plane, Klouser and Xanthy were continuing their hunt. The portal door had opened in an upmarket suburb. There were enormous houses in the street they were walking down. Xanthy could tell that Klouser was growing more and more angry, impatient and frustrated by the minute. Instead of trying to calm him down, she made him more angry.

"Looks like those two can't just outrun us. They fight like warriors."

"What?!" Klouser replied as he stopped in the middle of the street and looked at her with an infuriated look on his face. "They might have managed to escape, but just because they saved their own asses doesn't mean they're any match for the two of us. They got lucky. They're not as powerful as us and we can easily defeat them in a fight, as soon as we find them!"

A home owner who was busy taking his dog out to do its business on his neighbor's front lawn heard the two. When he saw them in the street and spotted their gutter blades, he grabbed his dog and rushed back into his yard. The sound of his footsteps drew their attention. Klouser and Xanthy pulled out their blades and ran towards the yard. They looked between the four cars parked in the front yard and in every possible place someone could've been hiding. Neither of them heard the home owner inside the house phoning the police. They made their way to the backyard, looked around for any sign of Kathy and Trent, and made their way to the next house's backyard. They continued searching the yards on that block for half an hour before heading back to the street.

Klouser was so busy venting his frustration that Xanthy could barely get in a single word. She wanted to suggest that they should move on to the next plane and continue searching there. A police patrol car was driving up the street ahead. It stopped when the officer spotted the two of them. Seeing the patrol car made Klouser stop bitching and complaining. Xanthy could tell by the look in his eyes that he wanted to vent his frustration in another way. The patrol car began driving straight towards them. Klouser's eyes and hands began glowing as he went down on one knee and held his palms an inch above the ground. Xanthy pressed her glowing hand against his back to give him some of her power. The patrol car stopped about ten meters in front of them and the officer was busy getting out of it when Klouser unleashed his destructive powers. The earth beneath their feet began shaking and streams of dim blue light came out of everything in front of him. The police officer tried to pull out his sidearm but dropped it as his energy was being drained from his body, along with the energy of everything around. Only a few streams of blue light came out of his body before he collapsed and his dead body began turning to nothing more than dust and bones. The sound of many people screaming made Xanthy smile. Most people in the houses thought it was an earthquake and some thought it was the Apocalypse. The street, the fancy cars, the fronts of all of the houses and the unlucky four residents who were outside in their front yards were torn apart and turned into nothing more than a mixture of sand and dust. Klouser could feel the energy he was draining out of everything and everyone he was destroying entering his body. It wasn't enough to satisfy his hunger for more powers. When he was done, he got up off his knee, turned to Xanthy, and said, "This won't do! I could destroy so much more and feed on much more energy when I have their powers."

"Then stop wasting time here and go look for them."

Xanthy opened a portal door and the two of them left that plane.

7

The place where the portal door had opened for Kathy and Trent was a perfect spot for them to continue with her training. It was a massive old abandoned industrial plant. Having been abandoned more than a decade earlier, the plant was full of old dilapidated workshops and warehouses. The rusty remains of old cranes, machines, scrap pieces of metal and other junk made the entire plant look like one big junk yard.

Trent was playing a game of cat and mouse with Kathy. He wanted to train her in a way that would prepare her for the next time Klouser and Xanthy found them. He was chasing after, using anything he could use his powers to manipulate as a weapon. Big pieces of scrap metal came flying straight at her. They all missed Kathy and struck the wall as she ran in through a door which led to what used to be a cafeteria. She ran in between the dirty remains of tables and chairs and when she looked back, she saw large pieces of scrap metal floating in the air as they came through the door, followed by Trent. Pointing his glowing hands at the pieces of metal, he looked at her and they smiled at each other before he attacked her. She held her arms stretched out to her sides and made six of the tables fly up into the air before she pointed at the pieces of metal heading straight at her and made the tables fly in between her and the metal. All this did was buy her time. The pieces of metal slowed down as they struck the tables and broke them apart, but they were still heading straight for Kathy. She pointed her hands at the pieces of metal and used her powers to try and gain control over them.

They kept moving back and forth between her and Trent. It appeared as if they were trying to see who of them was more powerful. Both of them quickly grew bored of doing this. She made the pieces of metal fly straight at each other and made them mangle together into a ball. Grinning confidently, she sent the ball straight back at him. It came flying at him so fast that he had to run out of its way as he tried to use his powers on it. He made it fly to the right and it crashed through the wall next to the door.

"That's better!" he said.

Kathy smiled as she ran up to him. Small bolts of energy flickered all over their hands as she took him by the hand.

"See, there's no such thing as too much fight training. You're getting better and better with your powers."

"That's because I have a good teacher," she said as she squeezed his hand and looked into his eyes. For both of them it felt as if time froze for a moment. Feeling the gentle touch of his hand and seeing the loving look in his eyes made her remember more of the memories she'd gained from her alternate selves. She could tell that he was looking at her and touching her in the exact same way he did with her alternate self that he'd fallen in love with. Intertwined with these memories were emotions she'd never felt for anyone ever before. She could tell by the way he stared into her eyes that he wanted to kiss her as much as she wanted to kiss him. He closed his eyes and bit his lip as he fought off the burning desire to kiss her. He feared that Kathy wouldn't feel the same way about him as her alternate self did.

"Come. Let's keep moving. We don't know where or when those two will show up again," he said.

She breathed out a quiet sigh of disappointment. She knew that what could've been a special tender moment for the two of them was lost. He raised his hand and was about to open a portal door when she stepped in front of him, and said, "Wait. Let me."

Trent smiled as he lowered his hand. Seeing her so eager to use her powers made him confident that the training was going well. She'd improved her fighting skills and gained full control over most of her powers, but it still took some extra effort and concentration for her to open a portal door. She pointed her glowing hand out in front of her as she walked through the hole in the wall. It didn't take her long to open a portal door right next to the big ball of mangled metal.

"See, you're getting better at this," Trent said.

"I have to do this more often. Then I might be as quick as you."

Before he could take Kathy by the hand, she wanted to test if she could use two forms of her powers simultaneously. While keeping the portal door open with one hand, she pointed her other hand at the big ball of metal and used her powers on it. The ball flew up into the air and broke a large part of the roof apart as it kept heading straight up into the air. Trent smiled as he put his hands on her hips, stared up at the ball as it headed higher and higher up into the air, and said, "See, you're getting better. We have to keep training until you can do all this and more with your eyes closed."

Kathy didn't allow the pleasant feeling of his hands on her hips, and his body pressing against her back, to break her concentration. After sending the ball of metal so far up into the air that neither of them could see it anymore, she finally took him by the hand and they ran into the open portal door. Shortly after the portal door had vanished back into the ground, it opened up again. Klouser and Xanthy came out through it. Both pulled out their blades as they began looking around. Xanthy was busy telling Klouser that she wished they could find Kathy and Trent, and finally bring their hunt to an end so that he could gain all of the powers he wanted. She was still busy speaking when the ball of mangled metal came crashing through the roof and fell through the floor only a few feet behind them.

CHAPTER IV

1

On another plane, the streets of an urban part of the city appeared to be filled with ghosts. To any planewalker who came to this plane for the first time, all the people and animals looked like ghosts because they were all partially transparent. When a portal door opened in the middle of a dirty side street, Kathy and Trent came stumbling out of it and fell on the small piles of garbage against the wall. He helped her up and they dusted themselves off before they walked down the side street. When they reached the busy street at the end of the side street, Kathy stared at all the people walking and driving past them. A young man with a wrapped package in his hands came running past her. She could see every detail of his face, his outfit, even the color of the paper the package he was carrying was wrapped in, yet she could still look straight through him and see the building across the street.

"What is this place? Is this almost like Limbo?" she asked.

Trent took her by the hand and kept looking around for any signs of danger as he replied, "Nope. They might look like ghosts to us, but all the people you see are alive and well on the Prime Physical Plane."

She looked at him, frowned and shook her head as she asked, "How is that even possible? If we're not on the Prime Physical Plane, how can we see the people?"

"We're not seeing the people. We're not seeing their bones, flesh, and blood. We're seeing their spirits. This is the Spiritual Plane. Stay close. There are lots of dangers here."

They began walking along the sidewalk. Kathy couldn't stop herself from staring at the souls of the people. Movement in the sky caught her eye and when she looked up, she stopped in her tracks and squeezed Trent's hand. He smiled as he looked at her, and said, "I was wondering how long it would take you to notice it. What do you think it is?"

She shook her head and couldn't think of an answer. What she was seeing was like something out of a horror film. There was dead silence. She couldn't hear a single voice or sound coming from up in the sky, yet she could see the war that was being fought there. High up in the sky, between the clouds, Angels and Demons were fighting their never-ending war for the souls of humans. Armed with golden swords, spears and shields, the Angels fought the Demons and sent many of the right back to Hell. Kathy could see flashes of blue light up in sky as portal doors were opening and more Demons were sent from Hell to continue fighting in the war.

"This is the war for the souls you see walking around you. It never ends. I've been here a few times and it gives me chills down my spine every time I see them fighting."

Trent looked around and saw something he wanted to show her. She was so awestruck by the sight of the Holy War in the sky that he had to kiss her on her cheek to get her attention. He took her to a parking lot in front of a grocery store across the street. Two men were standing behind one of the parked cars and it appeared as if they were arguing with each other. Kathy could see two blurry shapes behind both men. Trent pointed at them and said, "Can you see them? Concentrate and see what's behind them."

She stared at the blurry shapes and concentrated until the shapes began taking form. Both men had an Angel and a Demon standing behind them. She couldn't hear what they were saying or shouting at each other but she could tell they were furious at each other for some or other reason. The Angels were trying to get the men to turn their backs and walk away, while the Demons were trying to tempt the men into resorting to violence. Kathy turned and looked at all the people who were walking past the parking lot. She could see that each and every person had an Angel and a Demon walking with them. She saw one man who was getting into his car parked across the street. She could see what looked like claws sticking out of his shoulders that were holding on to his head, and the Angel was holding on to one of these claws, trying to pull the Demon that was possessing this man out of him.

"Scary, isn't it? People living their day to day lives unaware that their souls are in danger."

Kathy agreed and asked, "When can we go back to the main plane?"

"You mean the Prime Physical Plane."

"Whatever you call it. Seeing all these other planes is enlightening and all, but we have to go back to our own plane sooner or later, right?"

"We as planewalkers don't have our own plane, as you call it. As important as the Prime Physical Plane is, it's our duty to protect all the planes. And, besides, the very next plane we get sent to might be the Prime Physical Plane, or we might only be sent there after we were sent to twenty or thirty other planes. We have no control over that."

"We better get going then. We don't know when those two are going to end up on the same plane as us."

Kathy pointed her hand at an empty parking spot and used her powers to open a portal door. He took her by the hand and they were about to jump into it when the silence around them was shattered by the sound of gunshots. Two bullets struck the car right next to them. The portal door vanished back into the ground as they ran for cover.

"What the fuck!" she yelled as they took cover behind a car. "Since when did spirits start carrying guns?!"

"That's no spirit!"

Two more shots were fired and the bullets struck the car they were hiding behind. On the other side of the street, one of the two cop drones came walking out of an alleyway with his gun in hand. Trent peeked out from behind the car and saw the cop drone walking towards them. He pulled his head back just in time before the drone fired two more shots. He pressed his hands against the car, and said, "Put your hands on the car!"

"What?! Why?!" Kathy replied. She wanted to attack the drone and kill him with her powers. She didn't know why Trent asked her to touch the car.

"Just do it!"

She pressed her hands against the car and felt Trent's powers moving through the car. He used his powers to attack the drone in the best way he could think of. The cop drone fired one more shot as from the sidewalk to the parking lot. Using his powers, Trent made all of the windows of the car shatter into tiny shards. Instead of falling on the ground, each and every shard moved through the air like a bullet and struck the drone in his face, chest, stomach, and legs. None of them could hear the people screaming as they ran away. The car's windows didn't just shatter and fly through the air in the Spiritual Plane. It also happened in the Prime Physical Plane. All the people who saw this ran away thinking that the car was haunted. Kathy could feel what Trent had done with his powers to make this happen. This was his way of giving her another lesson on how to use her powers better. The cop drone was badly hurt. Most of his body was covered in blood from all his wounds. Clearly this didn't stop him. He fired the remaining bullets in his gun at the car before he began reloading it. Trent pulled out his blade as he ran out from behind the car and attack him. Kathy did the same. The two of them slashed and stabbed him until he dropped down on his knees. He raised his hand in a futile attempt to stop the blade only to have Kathy slash it off at the wrist. Trent slashed the back of his neck open and used the hook-shaped part of his blade to tear open his back straight down the middle. He grabbed the back of the drone's bleeding neck with his bare hand and pressed his fingers deep into the open wound. There was a faint blue glow in his entire arm and upper body as he used his powers to increase his physical strength. Kathy couldn't believe how easy he made it look when he effortlessly ripped out the drone's entire spinal column – unplugging him. The cop drone's limp dead body collapsed and there was blood squirting all over the place. Seeing this made Kathy's stomach turn. Trent tossed the bloody spinal column aside and turned to Kathy. Seeing the expression on her face, he said, "It's brutal but necessary. You get used to it after you've done it a few times."

She couldn't believe how calm he appeared. She stood frozen, staring at him and what remained of the drone. He looked at all the blood on his hand and held out his other hand before he said, "Come. Let's keep moving."

She shook her head one more time before she took him by the hand. She opened a portal door and they moved on to the next plane.

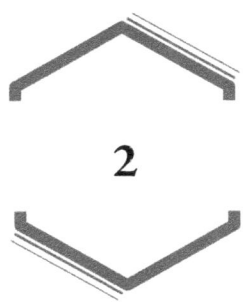

2

In a quiet subway, four friends were laughing and joking about a fight they witnessed at a bar earlier. On their way home after a night out, all of them were too intoxicated and too busy talking to notice the young man who was rummaging through the garbage in a garbage can. Down on his luck after being retrenched, the young man had too much pride to ask for help from family and friends, and resorted to looking food in the garbage. He saw the four friends as they got onto the train. He wanted to ask them if any of them had any spare change, but thanks to his pride, he chose to continue digging through the garbage. His face lit up when he found a half eaten toasted cheese sandwich. He took it out of the garbage can and was about to take a bite when a portal door opened right next to the garbage can. He ran away right before Kathy and Trent came out through the portal door. After helping her up off the ground, the first thing she asked was, "Is this it? Are we back on the Prime Physical Plane?"

Trent looked around, paused, closed his eyes, took a deep breath and shook his head.

"Nope. We're not there yet."

"What? How do you know?" she asked, sounding surprised.

"You just know. You feel it. Whether your on an alternate physical plane or some other plane, you keep getting that uneasy feeling in your entire body. When you're back on the Prime Physical Plane, you just feel like you're back where you belong. You'll feel it too."

He looked around and saw the crumpled up newspaper pages in the garbage can. He took them out and began using them to clean the blood off his hand. Kathy kept looking around for any signs of danger. With her back turned to Trent, she heard him toss the crumpled up newspaper pages back into the garbage can. She froze for a split second when she heard him pulling his blade out. She quickly pulled her blade out and turned around just in time to block Trent's blade with hers. Not seeing any signs of danger around, Trent thought that this was the perfect opportunity to surprise her with more fight training. As the two fought, he said, "Always – be ready – for a fight."

She could tell that he wasn't holding back. He was fighting her like he would fight Klouser or Xanthy. Seven minutes into their training session, both paused when they heard the sound of a train approaching. They put their blades away and quickly made their way out of the subway.

The street was quiet. There were three people walking on the other side of the street, and there was a young woman sitting at a bus stop busy smoking a joint. Kathy and Trent kept looking around as they walked past her. When they reached the corner of the street, Kathy paused and looked at Trent.

"What's wrong?" he asked.

"You were right. I can sense that we're not on the Prime Physical Plane. I can feel I don't belong here, and I'm not talking about the neighborhood."

"You're getting that uneasy feeling in your body, right? You're senses are adapting and changing thanks to your powers."

They crossed the street and looked for the nearest alley. When they found an alley, he opened a portal door and they moved on to the next plane.

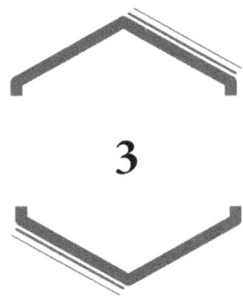

3

On an abandoned farm, many miles from the city, everything still looked in a good condition. The previous owner of the farm struggled through hard times for more than four years before he and his wife decided to sell all of their animals and the farm, and move to the city. The new owner of the farm owned two more farms. He was planning on starting a pig farm there the following month.

A portal door opened between the tool shed and what used to be a sheep pen. Kathy and Trent came out through the portal door and fell on a patch of grass. The first thing she did after she'd gotten up was to try and sense if they were back in the Prime Physical Plane. While she did this, Trent pulled out his blade and held her by the hand. There weren't any lights on anywhere. It was pitch black all around them. He tried to listen for any sounds of movement.

"I can sense that this isn't it either. We're not home yet," she whispered.

"I don't know where we are but we should keep moving. It's too dark for you to do more training here. When we reach the next plane, we should – "

The sound of gunshots shattered the peaceful silence of the night. Kathy and Trent ducked for cover as they ran to the back of the tool shed. Neither of them could tell where exactly the gunshots were coming from.

In the pitch black darkness, the second cop drone stood on the steps in front of the farm house's front door. He fired two more shots in the area where the portal door had opened.

Kathy and Trent remained dead silent and motionless as they tried to listen for any sounds of movement. She could feel the chill running down her spine when she heard the sound of footsteps coming towards them. She pulled out her blade. Trent squeezed her hand before he let go. The cop drone was walking blindly in the dark towards where the portal door had been. He pointed his pistol in random directions and fired. One of the bullets went straight through the tool shed and missed Kathy's head by mere inches. The cop drone kept pulling the trigger even after he'd fired the last bullet in his pistol. Hearing the clicking sound of the empty pistol, Kathy and Trent knew now was the time to attack. Trent used his powers to make his hand glow bright enough for them to see as they ran around to the front of the tool shed. The cop drone was busy reloading his pistol when Kathy's blade slashed off his fingers. She slashed him across the chest and stomach four times before Trent stabbed him in the chest. The cop drone dropped down on his knees. With his fingerless right hand, he reached out for his pistol on the ground in front of him. Trent slashed him across the chest one more time before he held his glowing hand above the cop drone's head, and said, "Do it! Finish him!"

Kathy hesitated for a split second before she raised her blade and slashed the back of his neck open. Her hands were shaking as she slashed his back open straight down the middle. The drone groaned in pain and hearing this made Kathy freeze. Trent knew that her first kill, her first attempt at unplugging someone, wasn't going to be easy for her. He also knew that it was something she had to learn how to do so that she would be prepared for if she ever had to fight Klouser or Xanthy.

"Unplug him! You know how to do it! Finish him!"

Kathy let out a short scream as she forced herself to dig her fingers into the flesh in the back of the drone's neck. She didn't notice it, but her eyes began glowing as she tapped into her planewalker powers. She ripped part of his spinal column loose and unplugged him. After the dead drone's face hit the ground, Trent pointed his glowing hand at Kathy. The look on her face as she looked at her bloody hand made it clear that she was in a state of shock. She couldn't believe what she'd just done.

"I... I pulled his... I killed him."

Trent hugged her and apologized for yelling at her.

She could feel the tears streaming down her face. The shock of having just killed someone in such a savage way left her hands shaking. What shocked her almost as much as the killing itself was how much power she felt throughout her entire body while she pulled out his spinal column.

"Come. Let's find a safe place. We can rest a little while you deal with the shock of what you just did," Trent said as he pointed his glowing hand at the farm house. Fearing that there might be another drone hiding inside the farm house, he told her to stay right behind him. She held her blade in her bloody shaking hand as she followed him. They made their way to the open front door. They paused on the steps and remained dead silent for a moment as they listened for any sound of movement coming from inside the house. Hearing absolutely nothing, they slowly entered the house. They made their way from room to room and didn't find any other drones. Breathing a sigh of relief, Kathy sat on the floor with her back against the wall next to a closet.

"This place is too clean," Trent said.

"What?" she asked, unsure of what he was trying to say.

"This place is too clean. It couldn't have been abandoned too long ago. The house is clean and everything still looks usable."

He pointed his glowing hand up at the light in the roof right above him. He walked to the switch on the wall right next to the door and flipped it, switching on the room's dim light. The glow in his hand faded away as he sat down next to Kathy.

"Unplugging another planewalker or a drone is never easy," he said.

"The power I felt throughout my body... The way that I knew exactly what to do... That doesn't shock me as much as the fact that I actually did it."

"You gained a lot of knowledge along with your powers. When you saw me unplugging that other drone, that awakened the knowledge in your mind on how to do it."

"I still can't believe I actually did it," she said as she shook her head and held her shaking hands together.

"Doesn't matter if it's Klouser, Xanthy, or one of their drones, when it comes to killing, remember that it's either us or them."

He moved closer to her and put his hand on her leg. She wiped the tears from her eyes, put her hand on his and looked at him. Seeing the look in his eyes and the expression on his face, she could tell that he was waiting for her to continue telling him how she felt so that she could get the feeling of guilt of her first kill off of her chest. She found it surprising that she could tell what he was thinking and what he was asking of her simply by looking at the expression on his face. She felt that she knew him better and was closer to him than anyone else she'd ever met before. She told him how she felt over her first kill and he kept reminding her that she had nothing to feel guilty about. He complimented her and told her that she had awoken the fighting warrior spirit inside of her. In an attempt to make her feel less guilty for doing what needed to be done, he told her that he was proud of her. As they got up off the floor, he said, "There isn't another way for us to defend ourselves from other planewalkers and drones. You'll learn to accept the brutal nature of unplugging our enemies."

Trent wanted to tell her that they should continue fight training when they get the chance to do so. He opened his mouth to speak but paused when she put her arms around him. The look in Kathy's tear-filled eyes as she stared into his eyes was one of mixed emotions. He could still see sadness and regret in her eyes as she tried to work through the emotional guilt she felt over her first kill. At the same time, he could see a look in her eyes that he hadn't seen in a woman's eyes for many years. A look of love. A look of desire for physical affection. As much as he felt the same emotions and desires for her, he was somewhat confused. He wasn't sure if what she was doing was coming straight from her heart, or if the shock from her first kill had left her so emotionally confused that she was doing this out of nothing more than emotional confusion. He opened his mouth and was about to tell her that they should probably move on to the next plane when she suddenly pulled him closer and kissed him. The surprise left him frozen for a moment before he put his arms around her and unleashed the emotions that were boiling inside his heart. The two kissed passionately. Neither of them wanted to stop or spoil the moment. While their lips were locked together and their bodies were pressed together, both of them forgot about the two psychopaths that were searching for them.

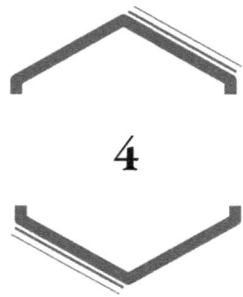

4

On another alternate physical plane, a portal door opened inside a storage room inside a convenience store. Klouser and Xanthy fell on top of boxes of chocolates in the corner of the room. Having heard the noise, the young man who was working the night shift in the convenience store came into the storage room and saw the two as they got up off of the boxes.

"You can't be in here! Get out! Go try and steal somewhere else!"

The young man ran to the counter and pulled out the baseball bat he kept behind the counter in case any customer tried to steal anything. He ran back to the store room. He was yelling at them to get out as he raised his bat and ran towards them when Klouser and Xanthy pulled out their blades. They made short work of him. Klouser slashed him across the chest and arms. Xanthy then slashed him across the side of his face and stabbed him multiple times in the stomach. He dropped his bat and blood came out of his mouth as he dropped down on his knees. Klouser gave him one last fatal slash across the throat before the two walked out of the storage room. Neither of them showed any emotions for just killing a man as they used the flag that was hanging on the wall to clean the blood from their blades. Before they left the convenience store, they stole a few snacks and cans of soda.

The street in front of the convenience store was quiet. Besides the few cars that drove past, they only saw two pedestrians who were walking on the other side of the street, each smoking a joint. Klouser and Xanthy kept looking around for Kathy and Trent as they made their way to the corner of the street. When they reached the corner, Xanthy opened the bag of chips she'd taken from the convenience store and began eating. Also feeling peckish, Klouser opened the box of doughnuts he'd taken and began eating one. After moving from plane to plane in search of Kathy and Trent for what felt to them like an eternity, both of them hadn't eaten in almost a full day. As they stood on the street corner eating, they kept looking around, wondering if their targets might be nearby.

"I wish we could just find them, kill them, get their powers and get all of this over with," she said.

"This hunt is taking a lot longer than I'd hoped. But don't worry. As soon as we find them, unplug them and take their powers, this hunt will be worth the effort."

For the following twenty minutes, they searched for Kathy and Trent in the alleyways and in a small abandoned shop. Both of them froze and looked at each other when they began making their way down another alley and heard voices. They pulled out their blades and slowly made their way towards the trashcans close to the middle of the alley. Thinking that it might be Kathy and Trent that were hiding from them, they prepared for a fight as they reached the trashcans. They thought the two were hiding behind the trashcans and were going to try to attack them at any moment. Klouser and Xanthy stopped and looked at each other with puzzled expressions on their faces when they heard what sounded like a man whispering something and a woman giggling. Klouser banged his blade against one of the trashcans. The noise made the married man and the prostitute who were busy having sex behind the trashcans rush to get up, pull their pants up and run as fast as their legs could carry them. Klouser laughed, shook his head and breathed out a frustrated sigh. He was disappointed that those two weren't Kathy and Trent. Xanthy was also frustrated. Unlike Klouser, her mind was wandering in a different direction. Klouser was wondering if Kathy and Trent were on this plane and, if so, where they should hunt for them next. Xanthy was also frustrated that they hadn't found their targets yet. She was also frustrated that she and Klouser had been so focused on the hunt that they hadn't been intimate with each other for a while. She groped his butt as they continued walking down the alley. When they reached the street at the end of the alley, she continued to touch and grope him to try and get his attention. He took little notice of her as he looked up and down the street and tried to decide where they should continue to search. Her sexual frustration was slowly turning into anger. They began walking up the dimly lit street and he was still so focused on the hunt that he completely ignored her when she shoved her hand down the back on his pants. She couldn't take it anymore. When they reached the next alley, she grabbed him and pulled him into it.

"Hey! You just could've said we should look for them here. What are you doing?"

She pushed him up against the wall, covered his mouth with her hand to shut him up and began unzipping his pants.

"The hunt can wait a few more minutes. I can't," she said before she took her hand off of his mouth and kissed him. Klouser was surprised by the intense passion in her kiss and the force she used to pull his pants down. As far as he could remember, she hadn't shown him that much love and desire since the first year of their relationship. Like two forbidden lovers, they made love in the alley.

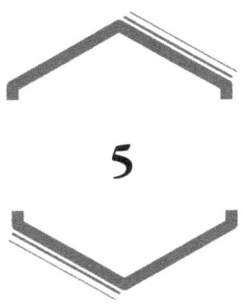

5

Kathy and Trent had also allowed their love and desire for each other to get the better of them. The two of them were making love on the floor in the farm house. What had started as nothing more than passionate kisses and gentle touches to each other's necks and faces had quickly turned into them undressing each other. The intense passion and pleasure they were sharing was so overwhelming to them that both of them forgot about Klouser and Xanthy. The possibility of being found and attacked by those two was the last thing on their minds as they made love. For more than an hour, they simply forgot about the rest of the world and satisfied each other's physical and emotional desires. Afterwards, they held each other and talked about how they wanted to start a life together once there was no one left to hunt them. Kathy talked about how she still wanted to explore other planes, and Trent talked about how he wanted to settle down somewhere in a small town close to forests and mountains. He began talking about how he'd like to have a small garden at their home one day when she got halfway on top of him, her breasts pressing firmly against his bare chest, and kissed him to silence him. She bit his lip before she got up and said, "We've been here a while. We probably have to move on."

Both of them were sad that they couldn't just stay there and fall asleep in each other's arms. As they were busy getting dressed, she told him that she liked his idea of getting a small house in a small town near a forest. While Trent was telling her of all the other planes he wanted to show her, something was happening outside.

A blue glow flickered in the ground in the pitch black darkness of night. A portal door opened. Trent saw the blue glow through the window.

"They're here!"

He and Kathy were still getting dressed in a hurry when Klouser and Xanthy came out through the portal door. Having had her sexual hunger satisfied on the previous plane, Xanthy was still smiling. When the portal door closed, both of them stared at the farm house. The light that was on inside the house made both of them pull out their blades. Klouser thought that the chances of Kathy and Trent being inside the house were slim. He thought that they might only find a lonely widower or a small poor family inside the house. Xanthy didn't care who they found inside the house, she just wanted to kill someone.

Kathy and Trent had finished putting their clothes back on and quietly tiptoed to the next room. She stayed close to the door while he tiptoed in the dark to the window. He peeked out through the window and saw nothing but darkness outside. He could hear the sound of footsteps coming towards the house. Kathy peeked out the door down the corridor at the front door. She saw Klouser for a split second as he kicked open the front door before she pulled her head back to avoid being seen. She quietly made her way across the room to Trent as he was slowly opening the window. Klouser and Xanthy stormed into the room where Kathy and Trent had made love. They froze when they saw the room was empty.

"There has to be someone here. Check the other rooms," he said.

Klouser made his way to the kitchen and switched on the light. He saw the door to the pantry at the back of the kitchen. Thinking someone might be hiding inside, he ran towards the pantry and rammed the door open. Xanthy came out of the master bedroom and entered the next room. When she switched on the light, she saw the window was wide open.

Kathy and Trent were running in the dark towards the tool shed. He was busy opening a portal door when Klouser and Xanthy came running out through the front door. Trent grabbed Kathy by the hand before they jumped into the open portal door.

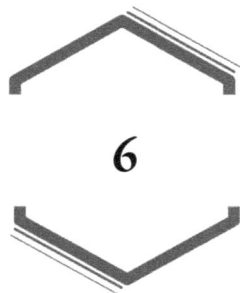

6

The remains of an old office building looked nothing like the place where billionaire business men and women once conducted their business. Everyone who'd once worked in that building was dead. The parts of the building that were still left standing were full of bullets holes.

A portal door opened in what was once a boardroom. Kathy and Trent came out through the portal door and fell on the rubble on the floor. A strong gust of wind blew a cloud of dust into the room through the large hole in the wall. They helped each other up and looked around at the rubble on the floor all around them. Trent pulled out his blade as he stepped closer to the hole in the wall. Kathy pulled out hers and followed him. He cautiously stepped out through the hole, looked up and down the street and stepped back into the building. When he looked at her, Kathy could see the fear-filled look in his eyes.

"I don't know this plane. I've never been here before," he said.

She stepped out through the hole and looked up and down the street. Her mind filled with fear and dread when she saw all the death and destruction in the street. A street that was once crawling with people, that was once filled with bumper to bumper traffic, and that once had office buildings, shops and stores on it was now a wasteland. As far as the eye could see, all of the buildings were either partially or completely destroyed. Between the rubble and the remains of destroyed vehicles in the street, there were dead bodies. She could see four dead soldiers and eighteen dead civilians on the sidewalk and between the rubble. When she saw the remains of a young woman who'd been savagely shot multiple times in the head and chest, the gory sight made her turn her head. That was when she saw the remains of a civilian who'd burnt to death in the car right next to her. The sound of an explosion in the distance made Trent pull Kathy back into the building.

"What is this place? So much death..." she said.

"Damned if I know. I've been to many planes but never this one."

Unbeknownst to them, the whole world was in the middle of World War Three on this plane. There was fighting going on in every city and town around the entire world. North, South, East and West. Even peaceful nations had no choice but to join the war and fight to protect their countries from invading forces. It all started when countries ruled by dictators and terror groups began attacking the US and other countries with weapons of mass destruction.

Trent was about to say that they should move on to the next plane. He took Kathy by the hand and that was when they heard the deafening sound of gunshots in the street. They were forced to run through the rubble to the next room as a few stray bullets came in through the hole in the wall.

Outside, a father and his thirteen year old daughter were running up the sidewalk. They took cover behind the remains of a car before they spotted the big hole in the wall of the building close to them. The enemy soldiers spotted them as they ran into the building. Armed with automatic weapons, each of the soldiers had a strange emblem on the backs of their dark gray uniforms. The emblem had a snake in the middle of it. Above the snake was the sun, below it was the moon, on its right was a scythe, and on its left was a sword.

Trent was about to open a portal door when Kathy heard the sound of the girl crying. She pulled out her gutter blade but quickly lowered it when she saw the fear-filled looks on the father and daughter's faces. They paused in fear when they saw Kathy and Trent. The sound of gunshots made them run past Kathy and Trent into what remained of the next room. The nine soldiers were firing in random directions as they ran into the building. Kathy and Trent took cover behind two large piles of rubble. The soldiers stormed into the room with their weapons blazing. None of them noticed how large and small pieces of rubble on the floor began glowing. Kathy and Trent used their powers to make pieces of rubble fly through the air. A large piece struck the first soldier straight in the face and crushed half of his head. The remaining eight kept firing but their bullets couldn't stop the pieces of rubble. All of them were either struck in the head, chest or stomach. One had his throat crushed by a small piece of rubble while the one right next to him was left with a gaping hole in his chest. Seconds later, all nine of them were dead. Trent grabbed Kathy by the hand and opened a portal door. He could feel her hand shaking as they left that plane. After the portal door closed and disappeared, there were drops of blood on the floor and on the rubble right in front of where the portal door closed.

7

The next plane they reached was yet another wasteland which had already been drained of all its energies. A portal door opened between two dunes. After Kathy and Trent came out through the portal door, he got up and looked around. He could see bits and pieces of destroyed buildings sticking out of the dunes. When he saw the skeletal remains of people in the sand right in front of him, he turned to Kathy and was about to tell her that this was another plane Klouser and Xanthy had destroyed and drained of all its energies when he saw she was still lying face down on the ground. He yelled her name as he dropped down on his knees next to her. He gently turned her body over and when he saw her face, her facial expression screamed: *'Pain! I'm in agony!'*

She let out a groaning noise as she looked down at her chest. Only then he saw the bullet wounds on her body. While they were killing the soldiers, two of their bullets had blasted through the rubble she'd taken cover behind. One had struck her in her chest and another had struck her in her stomach. Kathy had been so focused on fighting the soldiers and escaping that plane that she didn't even feel the bullets hitting her.

"Stay calm, Rosebud. Remember, these wounds can't kill you."

"Can't kill me, but still fucking hurts!"

She could feel both bullets moving inside her body as her powers were slowly forcing them out through the entry wounds. The pain she felt was so excruciating, she screamed and pressed her hands against the bullets wounds. She could feel both bullets as they came out and touched her hands. Her powers slowly began to numb her pain as her bullet wounds and the injured organs inside her body began to heal. Trent told her to stay down until the healing process was done but she got up. What she did next left him completely dumbstruck. She stumbled two steps back as she pulled out her blade, and said, "Perfect place for more training."

"What? More training? Now?"

As crazy as she knew it sounded to him, she still didn't feel the need to explain herself to him. She felt that to do training right after healing her injuries would be a perfect way to prepare her for their next battle. Trent was still busy pulling out his blade when she attacked him. He pulled out his blade just in time and sparks flew when their blades clashed right in front of his face. They fought for more than twenty minutes. During this time, he could tell that she was becoming a great fighter. He could tell that she wasn't resisting her powers anymore. As happy as he was that she was so eager to train and to use her powers, he still feared that her eagerness might make her cocky. During their training blade fight, he noticed four times that she held back on her attack. She swung her blade at him, he blocked it with his, grabbed her by the arm and pulled her closer. Standing nose to nose, he told her, "You're embracing your powers and fighting like a true planewalker, but I know you're afraid. I know you're holding back."

She took a step back and lowered her blade. She knew what he was saying was true.

"I know I'm gaining more control over my powers. I can feel in every inch of my body. I'm getting better with my blade too. I want to fight them and get this nightmare over with. But, if we have to face those two, I don't know if I have what it takes to beat them."

"You don't know? Not knowing, not ascending to the point that you know in your heart and mind that you are ready to face them is the quickest way you get your ass unplugged."

Knowing that he was right, Kathy paused before she replied, "We can't keep running."

"Until you fully ascend, the best thing we can do is stick together, keep moving from plane to plane and keep training. I hate to say it but I know how you feel right now. You feel brave and powerful on the one hand and scared shitless on the other. All these powers and mixed emotions leave you confused and that's what could get you unplugged."

She hated to admit it but she knew he was right. She was about to swallow her pride and tell him that she knew he was right when a portal door opened right next to them. They grabbed each other by the hand and began running. Klouser and Xanthy came out through the portal door and fell on the sand. Having hit the sand face first, Klouser was dazed, had a bleeding nose and a mouth full of sand. He was busy spitting out sand and rubbing his nose and forehead when Xanthy spotted Kathy and Trent making their way up a dune.

"Get up! There they are!" Xanthy yelled as she got up and began running after them. Still dazed, Klouser also got up and ran like a drunk.

Kathy and Trent made their way to the top of a dune. As Xanthy was starting to make her way up that dune, she pointed her glowing hand up at them and used her powers to blow the sand out from underneath their feet. Kathy and Trent were both sent tumbling down the other side of the dune. Both of their bodies slammed against one of the many burnt out vehicles at the bottom of the dune. Dazed, Trent picked up his blade and got up. Kathy was still down. Having hit her head against the car, she wanted to get up but the world was still spinning around her. She was so dazed that when she tried to pick up her blade, she grabbed a handful of sand instead.

"Get up! Come on! They're coming!" Trent said as he tried to help her up. He looked over his shoulder and saw Klouser and Xanthy making their way down the dune towards them. He turned around and raised his blade, ready to fight to the death to protect Kathy. Klouser pointed his hand at the car and used his powers to make the entire roof come off of the car and wrap around Trent's entire body. Trent screamed in pain as he fell over. He fought through the crushing pain he felt all over his body and tried to use his powers to free himself. On her hands and knees, still dazed, Kathy looked up when she heard him scream. Xanthy ran up to her and said, "Heads up," before she punched her in the face. The first punch left her with a bleeding lip. She grabbed her blade and tried to get up. As soon as she was on her feet, Xanthy punched her so hard that her entire body flew over the hood of the car. Trent was frantically struggling to free himself. Klouser pointed his blade at him and laughed before he attacked him. Trent's eyes glowed as he let out a deafening scream. He used his powers to make the roof of the car break apart. He freed himself just in time and dodged Klouser's blade before he began fighting back.

Xanthy laughed as she jumped on the hood of the car and looked down at Kathy. Standing on her hands and knees, Kathy looked up at her. Hearing Xanthy laughing at her, combined with the fear inside her mind, made something inside her snap. Xanthy stopped laughing when she saw how brightly Kathy's eyes began to glow. She raised her blade and was about to jump off the car when Kathy used her powers to make the hood fly off of the car, taking Xanthy along with it. Xanthy's body was slammed against the side of another car about thirty feet from where Trent and Klouser were fighting. The men were unleashing all their inner rage and the immense hatred they had for each other as they fought. Besides fighting each other with their blades, they used their powers to turn random objects around them into weapons. Klouser used his powers to send a human skull flying through the air straight at Trent's head. He shattered it into pieces with his blade and used his powers to send the wheel of a car flying through the air. Klouser was struck on the chest and sent flying through the air.

Kathy attacked Xanthy with her blade. As hurt as she was, Xanthy didn't let a little pain and blood stop her from fighting like a mad bitch.

She was yelling insults as she slowly drove Kathy back towards one of the cars. She blocked Xanthy's blade, punched her in the face, pointed her hand at the car right next to her and used her powers to make the car's front door fly off of the car. Xanthy was struck by the car door and sent flying through the air.

As they fought, Klouser tried to stab Trent. He moved out of the way but the blade still cut him across the side of his chest before it stabbed into the door of the big truck behind him. Before Klouser could pull his blade out of the door, Trent began punching him in the face and slashing him across his chest.

Kathy attacked Xanthy before she could get up off the ground. For a brief moment, Kathy believed she was going to beat her and unplug her right there and then. Xanthy slashed her leg and her stomach before she got up and angrily attacked her. She didn't think Kathy would be such a formidable opponent with the blade and she was growing angrier by the second just because she didn't turn out to be an easy target.

Klouser's forearms had several deep cuts on them from Trent's blade. He kept punching at him and kept blocking his blade every time Trent tried to slash at his neck. He used his powers to pull his blade out of the truck's door and fought back.

"You think you can beat me!" Klouser yelled.

He and Trent slashed each other numerous times, punched and kicked each other. Both of them thought that this was it: the final showdown, the last confrontation. In their minds, they were convinced that the only two possible outcomes for this fight would either be victory or death.

Kathy slashed Xanthy across her left cheek. She tried to stab her in the throat but her blade was blocked, Xanthy grabbed her by the wrist, forced her blade down and stabbed her in the stomach. Kathy pulled her hand free from her grip, punched her in the face and the two continued fighting. Every move she made made the pain in her stomach worse. With one hand on her bleeding wound she fought through the excruciating pain she was feeling and kept fighting, determined to bring this nightmare to an end.

Klouser was so high on the adrenalin flowing through his veins and the thought that he was going to win this fight at any moment that he didn't even feel the pain of all the bleeding cuts on his body. He blocked Trent's blade with his and punched him straight in the face. Trent's body slammed against the side of a car. He pressed his hands against the side of the car and used his powers to make two of the wheels come off of it and sent them flying straight at Klouser. Klouser used his powers to send one of the wheels flying straight up into the air but he was too slow to do the same to the second one. The wheel struck him straight on his chest, breaking two of his ribs on impact before sending him flying through the air.

Xanthy could hear Klouser screaming as he flew through the air and she heard the noise of his body being slammed against the side of a car, but she didn't even glance his way. She was too busy fighting Kathy and too determined to kill her to give a shit what was happening to Klouser. All of the fighting was starting to take a toll on Kathy. Not having gained full control over all her powers yet, she wasn't as ready for a fight for her life as she'd thought she was. She was still giving this fight her all and managed to slash and stab Xanthy a dozen times, but it was as if Xanthy could sense that this fight was making her weaker and weaker by the minute. Kathy took a swing at Xanthy's head with her blade. Xanthy blocked it with her blade, punched her in the face and kicked her in the stomach. Kathy stumbled backwards and fell flat on her back. Gripping her blade tightly in her bleeding hand, she lifted her head and saw Xanthy slowly walking towards her. To Xanthy, this fight was over and Kathy's powers were as good as hers. Seeing the cocky smile on her bleeding face made Kathy feel the hate in her boil. Her hate and rage for Xanthy and Klouser combined with her love for Trent made her fight through the pain. She wasn't going to give up the fight just yet. She could feel the indescribable pain from the stab wound in her abdominal area as she lifted her upper body off of the ground just far enough to point her glowing hand at the sand beneath Xanthy's feet. Sand flew through the air as Xanthy began to sink deeper and deeper into the sand. Using her powers, Kathy was making the sand fly out from underneath Xanthy's feet, and as soon as she was waist deep in the sand, all the sand that had flown out from under her feet came right back down into every gap around her legs, leaving her stuck in the sand. At first she panicked as she tried to free herself.

Trent came running up next to Kathy, helped her up and they began running away. Seeing them run, Xanthy used her powers to free her body. Sand flew through the air until she could climb out of the hole. Klouser came towards her. He tried to run but couldn't. He was bleeding, limping and badly injured. Injured or not, he didn't want Kathy and Trent to escape. He and Xanthy began chasing after them. At the bottom of another dune, Kathy and Trent made their way to the opening between a car and a van. He pointed his hand at the opening between the two vehicles and used his powers to open a portal door. He grabbed Kathy by her hand and they jumped into the portal. By the time Klouser and Xanthy reached the car and van, the portal door was already closing.

CHAPTER V

1

On an empty street, a portal door opened right next to what used to be a convenience store at an old abandoned gas station. Kathy and Trent came out through the open portal door and fell on the garbage that covered the ground. Neither of them moved a muscle to look around and see if anyone saw them or the portal door. They were bleeding and in too much pain to give a fat flying fuck if anyone had seen them. Kathy looked at all the bleeding wounds on her body. The sight of it combined with the pain she was feeling had her convinced she was dying. Also in pretty bad shape, Trent scraped together enough energy and fought through the pain to lift his hand and put it on her leg. Unbeknownst to him, he was putting his hand on one of the many bleeding cuts she had on her body.

"It... It feels like I'm dying," she said.

"Try to relax and take your – "

"I can't relax when my body feels like it went through a meat grinder."

Trent fought through the pain, got on his hands and knees, and crawled closer to her. He sat down next to her and put his hand on her forehead.

"As I was trying to say, try to relax and take your mind off of the pain. Your wounds are healing."

He gently touched her face and spoke about the fight they'd just had with Klouser and Xanthy to try and take her mind off of the pain she was feeling. It took a while for her wounds to heal. By the time her wounds were fully healed, Trent had already forgotten where on his body he'd been slashed and stabbed. He helped her up and they walked to the street. Standing on the sidewalk, they looked up and down the empty street. As they were looking at the sad state of the buildings in the street, he kissed her on the side of her head and whispered, "I told you you weren't ready to face them yet."

She put her arms around him and hugged him. Neither of them were aware that someone was staring at them. In a narrow opening between the convenience store and a small storage building, the pedestrian drone was looking for something to use as a weapon. He picked up a sharp five inch long piece of scrap metal that was between various other garbage in front of him and began sneaking towards them.

"Street might be quiet but we'd better get out of sight before those two find us again," Trent said.

Just as they turned to their right and began walking towards the nearest side street, the pedestrian drone attacked them. He cut the back of Trent's head and knocked both him and Kathy down before he jumped on top of her and tried to stab her with the piece of metal. She grabbed him by the wrists and tried to push him away. Trent grabbed him from behind and pulled him off of her. The drone hit him in the stomach with his elbow, turned around, punched him in the face and stabbed him in the chest with the piece of metal. He knocked the piece of metal out of the drone's hand and was about to pull out his blade and unplug him when the drone began punching him in the face. Dazed by the blows to the face, he began swinging his fists like a mad man and began punching back. Kathy got up. She pulled out her blade and was about to attack the drone from behind when she saw the parking meter right next to her. She put her glowing hand on top of the parking meter and yelled at Trent, "Get out of the way!"

He punched the drone four more times before he ran to the middle of the street. Using her powers, Kathy made every single coin come out of the parking meter. Each coin flew through the air and struck the drone like a bullet. Most of the coins tore straight through his body. When he turned to run away, she used her powers to make the entire parking meter break out of the sidewalk and fly through the air like a short, thick spear. The drone made a strange loud groaning noise when the parking meter tore through his body. Trent ran up to the drone and unplugged him. He ran up to Kathy, grabbed her by her hand – which was still glowing – and said, "We've gotta keep moving."

They ran down the sidewalk to the nearest side street and ran down it. Neither of them heard the sound of footsteps of someone following them down the dark side street. A tall dark figure ran in the shadows and he was carrying a gutter blade.

For more than fifteen minutes, Kathy and Trent ran from one side street to the next until they were both out of breath and they stopped to rest.

"We can't stay here for too long," he said. "We can catch our breath for a minute and then look for a safe place to hide for a while before we move on to the next plane. We don't know when those two are going to track us down again."

"I... I wish I had full control over my powers. I can feel it inside me, growing stronger."

"Just be patient. You'll know when you're done ascending and when you have full control over all your powers."

"We could've killed them both if I had full – "

"Planewalkers!" an unfamiliar voice yelled from out of the shadows.

Kathy and Trent pulled out their blades thinking it might be Klouser. They could both sense the planewalker powers of the stranger who was slowly walking towards them in the shadows. When he stepped into the dim light of a streetlight, they saw the stranger was holding his blade high above his head with both hands. He stopped and said, "Planewalkers, I'm like you and I mean you no harm."

Kathy and Trent kept their blades raised and remained prepared for a blade battle. After their battle with Klouser and Xanthy, neither of them were willing to take any chances.

"My name is Gregory. I'm a planewalker like you," he said before he slowly lowered his blade and put it back in its sheath. Kathy and Trent remained silent as they stared at him. He was tall, looked to be in his late thirties, and wore a dirty gray overcoat. She looked at Trent and whispered, "I thought you said there weren't any more planewalkers."

Trent shook his head in disbelief as he replied, "That was what Klouser and Xanthy told me when I worked for them. They told me that almost daily to print it into my mind that we were the last few left, and that it wouldn't take us long to hunt down the few that were still running from us."

Gregory lowered his hands and sat down on a trashcan before he said, "So those two are still alive. The rest of us have been waiting for other planewalkers to enter our plane and bring us the good news that both those fuckers had already been unplugged."

"You've heard of them?" Trent sounded surprised.

"Who hasn't? Every planewalker in my clan has joined me, fearing for their lives, fearing they won't gain full use of their powers and be strong enough to face those two if they ever managed to find our lair."

Kathy looked at Trent. The expression on his face made it clear to her that, just like her, he wanted to ask this man a million questions and didn't have the foggiest idea where to start.

Gregory could tell that both of them were too stunned to think straight.

"If you two are running from Klouser and Xanthy, you're more than welcome to join me and my clan at our lair."

Trent thought about it for a moment before he shook his head. Gregory and Kathy both were surprised that he didn't want to go to a safe place. Gregory thought he might suspect that he and his clan were as power-hungry and bloodthirsty as Klouser and Xanthy.

"We aren't like them. We embrace each other's development and help each other practice using our powers. We don't unplug anyone either," Gregory said.

"Thanks but no thanks," Trent replied.

"What? Why not?" Kathy asked, sounding shocked by his decision.

Trent looked at her, looked at Gregory, and said, "As far as Klouser and Xanthy know, we are the only planewalkers left. I... no, both of us appreciate your invitation to join your clan, but we can't risk Klouser and Xanthy finding more planewalkers. They'd hunt all of you down and unplug you all for your powers. If they get any more powers, then we would never be able to defeat them."

Kathy knew he was right. As inviting as the thought was to join a clan of planewalkers, she realized that they would be putting all their lives in danger. Trent looked deep into her eyes, and said, "I swore to protect you and help you gain full control over your powers. I don't know how long we have to keep moving from plane to plane, or how long it'll take you to gain full control over your powers, but until you do, until we can somehow stop those two, we only need each other."

Gregory nodded his head. He didn't take their rejection of his invitation as an insult. He realized that they had their own plans for the future and he wished them luck before he got up off the trashcan and began walking away.

"Wait... Could we meet the rest of your clan?" Kathy asked.

Trent was about to tell her that they shouldn't, but the idea of meeting other planewalkers made him pause, look at Gregory, and ask, "Would you mind? We don't want to intrude and we don't want anything other than to meet others like us."

Gregory smiled and said, "As long as you never tell anyone where our lair is, you're welcome to come and meet the clan."

They followed him down the side street and they began talking about how dangerous and powerful Klouser and Xanthy were.

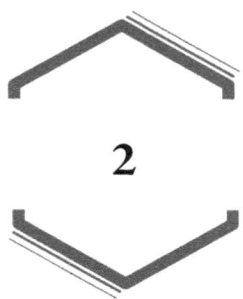

2

After walking and talking for twenty minutes, they reached one of the poorest suburban areas in the city. Most of the houses were in a horrible condition: half broken down, weeds growing all over the place, and piles of garbage as far as the eye could see. Kathy and Trent both kept one hand on their blades just in case Gregory was leading them into a trap. He seemed honest and genuine but they weren't going to take any chances.

Gregory led them to a street that looked like something out of a war zone. There were massive potholes in the street, the sidewalks on both sides of the street were lined with garbage, and all of the houses looked uninhabitable. He led them to one of the houses and warned them not to fall into the deep hole in the front yard. It was too dark for them to see it, so they followed close behind him. It was too dark for them to see what the front of the house looked like. All of the windows were boarded up and the pile of scrap metals and bricks on the front porch, right in front of the front door, served as a barricade. Kathy and Trent followed him to a narrow path between the house and what little remained of the garage. The dim light above the backdoor provided them with enough light to see the state of the backyard: there was a tool shed and two vegetable gardens against the back wall with a small chicken coop between them.

Gregory knocked on the backdoor. Kathy saw a faint glow through the window right next to the backdoor. A skinny lady pulled the curtain back inside the house and looked to see who was knocking.

Kathy saw that the glow was coming from the woman's palm. She stared at Kathy and Trent for a moment before looking at Gregory. He nodded at her and she unlocked the backdoor. The skinny lady was Gregory's wife. She greeted him with a kiss and stared at Kathy and Trent, waiting for him to introduce them. He merely pointed at them, and said, "These two are also planewalkers. They didn't come to stay. I just want to introduce them to the rest of the clan."

"Who says they aren't working for Klouser and Xanthy. If they're not here to join us, they might be here to spy on us," Gregory's wife said.

"Listen, if you guys are uncomfortable with us being here, we'll leave," Kathy said.

"Nonsense. You two could've unplugged me when I approached you. I trust you," Gregory said.

Gregory's wife kept giving Kathy and Trent a look that screamed: *'I don't fucking trust you'* as they entered the house. There were two small tables in the middle of the kitchen with fourteen soup bowls and a loaf of bread on one of them. On the stove, there were three big pots of pea soup busy cooking. Kathy and Trent followed Gregory to the living room. Gregory's wife followed close behind them, ready to use her powers if they posed any threat to the clan. The living room looked like a storage room. There was a large freezer in the corner and five big cupboards – made out of scrap pieces of wood and metal – that were filled with food and supplies. Gregory stepped into the hallway and opened a door. The door led down to the large underground bunker underneath the house where the rest of the clan hid most of the time. He called out to everyone in the bunker and asked them to come upstairs. The twelve other planewalkers came to the living room one by one. All of them appeared to be afraid when they saw Kathy and Trent. Clearly they weren't used to strangers being invited into their lair. Kathy was surprised to see how many they were. She was equally surprised to see how young most of them were. Gregory introduced her and Trent to the rest of the clan. The oldest member of the clan – a man in his late forties – stepped up to Gregory and asked him why he brought them there.

"These two are fighting Klouser and Xanthy."

Gregory's words received mixed reactions from the rest of the clan. Most of them laughed because they thought Klouser and Xanthy could never be defeated. Others stared at Kathy and Trent with an expression of awe and admiration on their faces. One of those who had laughed stepped forward and looked at the two as if he was examining them.

"You guys really think you can take down the two baddest planewalkers alive? Either you got bigger balls than the rest of us, or you guys are just totally fuckin' looney," the skeptic said.

Gregory grabbed him by the back of his coat, pulled him back, and whispered, "That's rude. They're braver than any of us, so quit the disrespect."

The skeptic nodded his head and apologized. Kathy and Trent ignored his apology and looked at the young man and woman who was hesitantly stepping closer to them. Both of them looked much younger than they were. At a glance, one wouldn't think that either of them were in their early twenties. Both of them looked as if they still should've been in high school. They stared at Kathy and Trent, struggling to find the words to ask the million questions that were running through their minds. The young woman's hand shook as she slowly held it out to Kathy. Unsure if the woman wanted to touch her or shake her hand, Kathy held out her hand to the woman. When she touched the palm of Kathy's hand with her fingertip, the blue glow made everyone in the room fall silent. The young man looked at Trent's hand, too scared to hold his hand out like the young woman did. Trent held his open hand out to the young man and, when he touched his palm, the young man's mouth hung open as he stared at the blue glow and felt how powerful Trent was.

"I can sense your powers. Do you think it'll be enough to beat Klouser and Xanthy?" the young man asked.

Trent looked at Kathy. He didn't know how to reply. To him, it felt as if this scared young man and the rest of the clan were expecting him and Kathy to defeat Klouser and Xanthy. He looked at everyone else in the room, saw how they were staring at him, and replied, "We might not be as strong as Klouser and Xanthy are, but they will be defeated. I can't say when or how. All I can say is that we'll make it our mission to make the planes safe for all planewalkers."

Everyone in the room, even the skeptic, smiled at the thought that they could regain their freedom soon. Kathy and Trent stayed at the lair for little under an hour before they left. Everyone wished them luck and Gregory told them to come visit if they ever ended up on their plane again. As they walked out of the front yard, Kathy groped Trent's butt, and said, "You just made a promise to those planewalkers. It's up to both of us to keep that promise."

"We will. I know we're running and hiding like cowards right now, but we'll have to face them and put an end to this sooner or later. It all depends on you and your powers. I could face them alone and do some serious damage to them both, but I'd still probably end up spineless and dead. We have no control over how fast you ascend. I pray it'll happen before we face them again."

"I wish it could've been easier to get control of all my powers. I can feel it inside of me, burning to be used, but every time I use it, I feel like I'm firing a fully loaded machine gun that could fall out of my hands at any moment."

"You're afraid of your powers. Shitty as it sounds, that's normal. The more you use your powers and your blade, the more it dawns on you that you have full control of your powers. When you get comfortable with your powers, or as you put it: the fully loaded machine gun in your hands, you'll be more powerful than you ever imagined. It's that feeling of power and the hunger for more power that turned Klouser and Xanthy into the monsters they are today."

"I won't get crazy with my powers. I won't turn out like them."

He looked at Kathy and squeezed her hand before he asked, "Are you sure? You tell yourself that now because you know the difference between right and wrong, good and bad. But if you let your powers control you instead of you controlling your powers, you'll start to crave more. I saw it when I worked for them. Klouser and Xanthy want more powers worse than a junkie wants his next high. I also felt the hunger for more powers while I was with them. Luckily I snapped out of it before the hunger totally consumed me and turned me into a monster."

He kissed her before they continued making their way down the dark streets in search of a safe place to hide for a while. They felt like they were walking in circles until they found an old abandoned scrap yard. The stench that hung in the air was awful. There were piles of scrap all around. Without any warning, Trent used his powers to make an empty soda bottle fly off of one of the piles. It struck Kathy on her butt. She turned around, smiled and knew what he wanted. He raised his hands, pointed at all the piles around them, and said, "Look at all these weapons around us. Anything you can use your powers on, you can turn into a weapon when we fight Klouser and Xanthy."

Kathy and Trent began another training session. They used their powers on the junk to attack each other and to block each other's attacks. Considering how their previous encounter with Klouser and Xanthy went, he knew she needed more training.

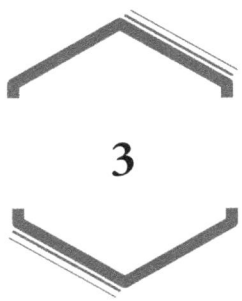

3

Klouser and Xanthy were on an alternate physical plane. To them, it felt as if they'd been hunting for Kathy and Trent for an eternity. He opened a portal door in the middle of an empty backstreet and they moved on to the next plane.

On the next plane, a portal door opened in the middle of a dirty dark street. After coming through the portal door, Klouser and Xanthy continued their search. When they reached the next dark street, they paused and pulled out their blades.

"I can sense them," she said.

"Me too. They must be nearby."

They could sense a planewalker, but it wasn't Kathy or Trent. Gregory stood in the shadows, hiding behind a piece of wall from what used to be a beautiful old house. His heart raced as he stared at them as they ran down the middle of the street. He began running back to the lair to protect the clan. Having sensed how powerful Klouser and Xanthy were, he hoped and prayed that they didn't find the lair, and that they didn't find Kathy and Trent.

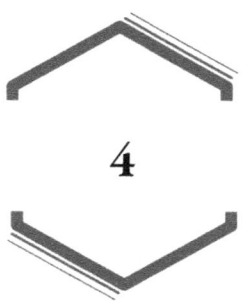

4

Kathy and Trent were out of breath when they finally stopped their training session. It had gone on much longer than he'd intended. During this training session, he'd fought her with all his might and used all his powers on her to prepare her for Klouser and Xanthy. The way she'd fought back with her blade and used her powers on numerous items of junk in the piles around them left him injured and impressed. Yet still he didn't believe she was ready to fight them. Was his love for her clouding his judgment?

"Impressed?" she asked.

"Yes. I'm impressed," he said as he leaned against a pile of junk to rest. "Just like the last time we faced Klouser and Xanthy, you've proven that you can fight and use your powers. I'm still fearful that the next time we're forced to face them, you might underestimate them and think that you can easily beat them. If you'd seen what I'd seen when I worked for them, they're powerful, heartless, ruthless, and kill without hesitation."

Kathy took a moment to catch her breath as she looked at the bleeding wounds she'd sustained during their training session, wiped the sweat from her forehead, raised her blade, and said, "That means you have to keep training me."

Trent smiled as he looked at her and shook his head while he said, "You're right. We have to keep training every chance we get. We've been on this plane for too long. We can continue your training when we move on to the next plane – "

He paused as he raised his blade and looked around. Kathy wanted to ask him what was wrong but then she too sensed the presence of a planewalker nearby.

A large rusty sheet of metal came flying through the air straight at Kathy's head.

"Get down!" Trent yelled.

Kathy glanced over her shoulder and saw the sheet of metal flying towards her. She dropped down on her knees just in time and the sheet of metal missed her head by less than an inch. Trent used his powers to send the sheet of metal crashing into a pile of junk. Klouser and Xanthy emerged from the shadows with their blades in hand. Trent's eyes and hands glowed brighter than ever before as he punched his fist into the pile of junk. Kathy ran towards him and covered her ears as he let out a deafening shout. Using all his powers, he turned the junk into a weapon. Each and every object on the pile began glowing as they flew through the air, straight at Klouser and Xanthy. They used their powers to send a few of the objects flying straight up into the air, used their blades to slash some of the objects to pieces, but they weren't quick enough to avoid being struck and injured by a number of the objects. Kathy dropped down on one knee next to Trent and punched the ground with her glowing fist. The spot where her fist struck the ground glowed neon blue as a crack in the ground traveled all the way from her fist to where Klouser and Xanthy were. They were still being struck by junk when the ground underneath their feet began to crumble. They fell into a shallow hole in the ground and Trent still kept sending junk flying at them. Injured, Klouser began using his powers to fight back. He held his blade in front of his face like a shield and used his powers to make it glow. Seeing what he was doing, Xanthy did the same. Some of the objects still struck them, but they used their powers to send most of the objects flying straight back at Trent. He had the wind knocked out of him when an old broken printer struck him in the stomach. Seeing him stumble backwards, Kathy looked at Klouser and

Xanthy, and saw that they were busy climbing out of the shallow hole. She punch the ground with both fists and used her powers to send an energy wave through the ground. A wide curved glowing line moved through the ground and knocked both of them back into the hole. She got up, pointed her blade at them and was preparing to use her powers to attack them again when Trent grabbed her by the hand and they ran away.

Dazed, Klouser and Xanthy got out of the hole and began chasing after them in the dark street. It was too dark for them to see Kathy and Trent. All they could hear was the sound of them running down the middle of the street. Klouser ran in front of Xanthy. He pointed his hands to his right and used his powers to make a wall in front of an abandoned house break apart. Large and small chunks of the wall came flying past Kathy and Trent, some missing their heads by mere inches. She could feel Trent tightening his grip on her hand before he pulled her to the left and they ran down a dark side street. They ran to an empty parking lot in front of what used to be a hardware store. The doors and windows were all boarded up. Trent led her to the main entrance doors and used his powers to break the doors and the boards apart. They ran into the building and both tripped over the junk that was on the floor. He pointed his glowing palm at her to see if she was injured. Before he could do or say anything, she got up and used her powers to open a portal door. Neither of them heard the sound of footsteps coming from outside. Out of breath, Kathy and Trent couldn't run towards the open portal door. They jogged. Klouser and Xanthy came running in through the door and saw the two jogging towards the portal door. They ran after them hand in hand. When Kathy and Trent jumped into the portal door, Klouser grabbed hold of Kathy's foot and all four of them disappeared into it.

5

On another plane, there was a seemingly endless hallway. There were strange ambient colors moving on the walls. Throughout the entire brightly lit hallway, there were no doors and no windows. This was the mental plane.

A portal door opened in the middle of the hallway. Instead of jumping out through the portal, all four planewalkers came hovering out of it. All of them were unconscious. As the portal door closed behind them, their bodies hovered two feet above the floor. Xanthy's body slowly hovered a few inches higher up into the air. The minds of Kathy, Trent and Klouser came out of their bodies. Their minds looked like smoke shaped like their faces. The minds of the three vanished into Xanthy's head.

Inside Xanthy's mind was what looked like an enormous room made out of skin and flesh. There were many doors all around the room, each made out of human bones, stained with blood. Moaning, groaning and crying noises could be heard coming from every door. Kathy, Trent, and Klouser's minds enter the room and hover around in a circle before each of them hover through a different door. Kathy's mind entered the room in Xanthy's mind which held all of her happy memories. The room had a wooden floor and there were images floating around of happy evil memories Xanthy had with Klouser. The pink walls of the room had bullet holes in it and there were large parts that were covered in blood. Kathy saw all the happy memories floating around her. The images she saw of Xanthy and Klouser having sex, and of the two savagely killing other planewalkers were disturbing. Her mind hovered to the nearest wall and she began looking for a way out of the room. As scared as she was to be in such a strange place, and as unsure she was of how she was going to get back into her body, she kept telling herself to be strong and not to give in to her fears. She remembered everything Trent had told her and she blocked out her fears and tried to find a way out.

Trent's mind hovered into a small dark room. This was where all of Xanthy's childhood memories were. He saw dozens of images from her childhood hovering in a circle. The first image he saw was of a seven year old Xanthy sitting on a dirty chair with a torn rag doll in her hands. He could see the tears in her eyes. The second image that caught his eye was of an eleven year old Xanthy looking for something to eat in a trashcan behind a bakery. The third image that came floating past him was that of a seventeen year old Xanthy sitting crying in a bathroom with a bleeding nose and a black eye after she'd been brutally beaten by both her parents for not bringing home any money. Trent's mind began looking for a way out of the room.

Klouser's mind hovered into a room in Xanthy's mind where all of her hopes and dreams were. He hated the bright cheerful colors on the walls. There were at least a hundred images floating in a circle in front of him. It was only when he saw his own face on most of the images that he took a closer look. He saw an image of him and Xanthy sitting on a beach drinking cocktails. The second image he saw was of the two of them covered in blood with Kathy and Trent's dead bodies on the ground in front of them. The third image was that of Klouser and Xanthy using their powers to kill normal humans. The fourth image was of the two of them sitting like royalty in a fancy dining room, eating from golden plates and drinking from golden cups. The next image he saw shocked him. He saw Xanthy in a big bed with a baby in her arms, and he saw himself standing next to the bed with a big smile on his face and a teddy bear in his hand.

All four their bodies still hovered above the floor. The dead silence in the endless hallway was shattered when Xanthy opened her eyes, gasped and let out a deafening scream. Her body stopped hovering and fell on the floor. She kept screaming and began rolling around on the floor, clawing at her own face, forehead and neck.

"Get out of my head!" she screamed. Kathy, Trent, and Klouser's unconscious bodies looked so peaceful as they hovered in the air while Xanthy was rolling around on the floor like a mad woman. She kept screaming as she began clawing at the top of her head and began tearing out her hair.

In Xanthy's mind, Kathy, Trent, and Klouser's minds were sucked out of the rooms they were in and forced into what looked like a maze filled with scary creatures. Every monster and scary creature she'd ever seen in her nightmares and in horror films were lurking in this maze. Kathy's mind moved between the images of hideous creatures as she looked for a way out of the maze. Trent's mind was doing the same. Klouser's mind was so overcome with fear that he didn't dare to move any closer to the images of beasts he saw before him. Kathy and Trent's minds find each other between the creatures. Together, they continued looking for a way out of the maze. The deeper they moved into the maze, the more it seemed as if they were moving in circles. They kept seeing the images of the same monsters over and over again. They reached a long corridor with many doors on both sides of it. Thinking that one of the doors might be a way out, they tried to open the first door but it wouldn't open. They randomly tried opening many of the other doors but not a single one of them would open. At the end of the corridor, they saw what appeared to be elevator doors. The doors kept opening and closing and the light inside the dirty elevator flickered bright red. They went into the elevator and the doors closed. They heard strange sounds coming from outside of the elevator. It sounded like voices whispering and people scratching on the outside of the elevator doors. The whispers slowly became screams and the scratching noises turned into banging noises. Fingers began poking holes in the elevator doors. Long, short, curved and straight human fingers and ugly green monster fingers were pointing at them. Kathy looked down and saw dozens of evil glowing eyes staring at them through the small holes in the floor. Trent saw the dim white flickering light of the elevator buttons and randomly began pushing them. Instead of numbers, every button just had an X on it. Kathy saw the glowing eyes began to disappear one by one. Thin slimy black tentacles came out of the holes in the floor and began wiggling around beneath her.

Klouser's mind finally moved between the scary images and he began looking for a way out. As scared as he was, he feared that he might be trapped in there forever if he didn't try to escape. The path he took led him to a corridor made out of human skin. There were hundreds of snakes moving around underneath the skin on the walls. He could hear the hissing sound of the snakes as he moved down the corridor towards the revolving doors at the end of the corridor. Each of the five revolving doors looked different. One looked in perfect condition. One was covered in mud. One had thousands of needles sticking out of it. One was covered in a glowing green slimy substance. And the last one had blood splatter on it. He picked the one in perfect condition and went through it. On the other side of it was one of Xanthy's worst nightmares. Klouser saw an image of Xanthy standing in front of a grave with his name on it. He didn't notice the tears streaming down the gray walls around him as he moved towards Xanthy. The image of Xanthy was unlike anything he'd seen before. He saw her sad and crying with a look of utter heartbreak in her eyes. He was too selfish and self-absorbed to realize that this was a sign that she really loved him. The first thing he thought of when he saw her like this was that it was a sign that she was emotionally weak.

Kathy and Trent's minds tried everything they could think of to get out of the elevator. The elevator doors finally opened and they moved out of it into a corridor that was filled with dead bodies. The bodies were all over the floor, hanging from hooks on the walls and from rusty chains on the ceiling. All of the bodies were in the advanced stages of decomposition. Most of them were covered in maggots.

Back in the mental plane, Xanthy was a bloody mess. She was still rolling around on the floor, screaming, clawing at her head. Her head, face and neck were covered in bleeding claw marks. She looked like a crazy woman who'd completely lost her mind and was trying to kill herself with her bare hands.

Kathy and Trent's minds moved between the dead bodies down the corridor. At the end of the corridor was a wall covered in rusty manhole lids. All of the manhole lids randomly opened and closed. Desperate to escape this hell, they moved closer, waited for one of the manhole lids to open and entered the pitch black darkness on the other side of it. Klouser was still staring at the image of a sobbing Xanthy when Kathy and Trent's minds came through the wall next to him. He instantly tried to attack them. His effort to harm them were in vain. When they tried to attack him, they also realized that they couldn't hurt each other in the states they were in. The walls around them lit up in a blinding white glow and their minds were sucked out of the room by an invisible force.

In the mental plane, blood came out of Xanthy's mouth as she screamed at the top of her lungs. Kathy, Trent, and Klouser's minds came out of her body and went back into their bodies. One by one, their bodies fell on the floor. They were disorientated and confused, and the sound of Xanthy's screams made them all panic. Trent glanced back at Xanthy. He was shocked to see how badly she'd injured herself. When he saw Klouser standing on his hands and knees, struggling to get back on his feet, he wanted to attack him. He and Kathy both were trying to get up, but they too ended up falling back down on their hands and knees. Kathy saw Klouser trying to get up a second time only to fall back down. She tried to pull out her blade. As much as her head was spinning and as confused as she felt, she still wanted to kill him. Her one arm gave way beneath her and she fell flat on her face. When Trent saw that Klouser was slowly getting back on his feet, he knew that they had to make a run for it. Neither of them were in any condition to try and fight Klouser. Still on his hands and knees, Trent pointed his hand out in front of him and used his powers to open a portal door.

"Come on, Rosebud!" Trent said as he began crawling towards the open portal door. He grabbed her by the arm and tried to pull her along as he struggled to drag his own body forward. She pulled her arm free from his grip, grabbed him by the hand, and they crawled into the portal door side by side. Klouser tried to stand up and fell back down on his butt. Only then he saw how badly Xanthy had injured herself. He glanced over his shoulder only to see how the portal door vanished back into the floor.

"Nooo!" he yelled angrily. "They got away again!"

Xanthy stopped screaming and sobbed. She'd injured herself so severely that the pain left her feeling as if she was dying. She looked at Klouser and held her bloody hand out to him, hoping he could do something to take the pain away. She knew that her wounds would take a while to heal. All she wanted from him was to do something, anything just to take the pain away.

"What have you done to yourself?" Klouser asked.

"K-Klouser... He-help me..." was all she could say before she coughed out blood. Having seen in her mind how much she loved him, having spent so many years with her in which she was devoted to him and their evil deeds, one would think that his love for her would make him do anything he could to help her, to comfort her while her powers slowly healed her wounds. Unfortunately for her, his love for power was far greater than any emotion which he'd ever felt for her. To him, that which he'd felt for her all along was far from love. For Klouser, she was his companion, she was his partner in crime, she was his bed buddy, but he never loved her. When she reached her hand out to him, he grabbed hold of her wrist and pulled out his blade.

"Wh-what are you d-d-doing?" she asked.

"I'm sorry baby. I can't wait for you to heal. I have to find and kill those two before she gains full control over her powers. Nothing should stand in the way of me gaining more powers. Remember? You taught me that."

Klouser pulled hard on her arm and flipped her body over. Lying on her stomach, she turned her head and tried to look at him as she said, "N-nooo... You can't... You b-b-bastard!"

He raised his blade and said, "I'll miss you when I have their powers. I'll miss you when I kill normal people for fun again, but mostly, I'll miss you in bed. You were always a great fuck. Bye baby."

She screamed and tried to get up. He slashed the back of her neck and her back open. He dropped down on one knee and began the gory task of unplugging her. As much as she tried to fight back, she was too weak and too badly injured to do anything. Seconds later, she let out one final scream before he ripped out her spinal column. Feeling all her powers enter his body burned away any traces of guilt he might have felt in the back of his mind. His lust for more power had pushed him so far over the edge that he didn't care who he had to betray or kill to gain more power. Klouser had finally revealed what a heartless monster he truly was. He got up off his knee, took a deep breath and took a moment to enjoy the feeling of her powers in his body. He looked down at Xanthy's dead body, grinned and said, "I'll take something to remember you when I face those two."

He took her blade. After opening a portal door, he left that plane and left her body behind like discarded garbage.

CHAPTER VI

1

A portal door opened in a place that had bright white mist as far as the eye could see. Kathy and Trent came out through the portal door and they fell on what felt like a soft smooth surface. Still feeling disorientated after their out of body experience on the mental plane, it took them a minute before they finally got up.

"What is this place?" she asked.

"I have no idea. Don't think I've ever been on this plane. Stay close."

They slowly and cautiously wandered through the mist until she noticed movement.

"I think there's someone over there," she whispered.

Trent stopped and tried to see what she was seeing. He also saw what looked like people walking through the mist.

"Stay behind me," he said.

They slowly moved closer to see what the people were doing. When they reached the spot where the people were walking, they noticed that there was a clear open path through the mist, along which many people were walking. Among those who walked past them, there was an elderly woman wearing pajamas, a young cop wearing his uniform, a young woman wearing coveralls, and a teenage boy wearing a snazzy suit, to name a few. It was only when they looked to their right that they saw where the people were going. The path led to the stairway to the Kingdom of Heaven. The golden glowing stairway led up to what looked like white clouds. They couldn't see the Gates of the Kingdom of Heaven above the clouds at the end of the stairway. Kathy and Trent looked at each other.

"Are... Are we where I think we are?" she asked.

Trent was about to answer her when the Archangel Michael appeared in front of them. He had long wavy light brown hair and had big white wings that matched his white outfit. He could sense their fear as they stared at him.

"You are not supposed to be here. It is not time for you to meet our Holy Father yet," he said in a calm voice. "Return to your world."

Kathy and Trent felt like they wanted to apologize but neither of them knew what to say. Trent opened the portal door. Michael smiled at them when they looked back at him before they jumped into the open portal door.

On a small secluded beach close to a small town, two stray dogs came walking along the path between the bushes which led from the street to the beach looking for something to eat. They froze in their tracks when they saw the glow of the portal door opening on the beach and ran back along the path when Kathy and Trent came out through it. The darkness of night around them, the feeling of the cold beach sand beneath them, and the sound of waves crashing close to them had a calming effect on them. Still holding each other by the hand, Trent squeezed her hand and was about to ask her if she was okay, when she said, "We were so close to Heaven just now. Did you feel what I felt while we were looking at that stairway?"

Trent let go of her hand and wiped a tear from his eye before he replied, "I felt calm. I felt like there wasn't a need to run and fight anymore. I felt a kind of peace in me I've never felt before."

"That's it. I felt like I was finally home."

They got up and made their way to the path between the bushes. They followed the path to the dimly lit street and when they reached it, Trent asked, "Did you see how bad Xanthy looked?"

"No."

"Don't know what happened to her but she looked like she fought a gang and lost."

Neither of them knew Xanthy was dead and that Klouser took her powers. They followed the street and reached the small town where they began looking for a safe place to hide for a few hours.

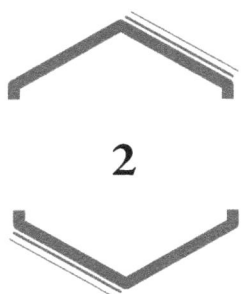

2

On another plane, Klouser was searching for them in the industrial area on the outskirts of the big city. Walking along a dark dirty backstreet with both blades in his hands, he could still feel his new powers in his body. Having gained Xanthy's powers, he felt untouchable and unstoppable. After searching for a little while, he began growing impatient and frustrated that he hadn't found them yet. It was as if, not that he was so powerful, he believed Kathy and Trent should be offered to him on a silver platter. His new powers had him feeling like he was so powerful and important that he should be given whatever he wanted.

Behind one of the factories, two security guards were sitting in a small room at the rarely used back entrance gate. Like every other boring night shift week that they worked together, the two men were talking about anything that came to mind just to pass the time. One was talking about how his son didn't like playing sports when the other spotted Klouser through the window. Shocked by the sight of the blades he was carrying, he interrupted his colleague, and said, "Check out this guy. What the heck is he carrying?"

Both security guards got up and stepped out of the room to see. Klouser spotted them and stopped when he reached the gate. They took out their flashlights and shined them on him.

"What the...? Sir, you can't be walking around at night with those swords. You'll probably get arrested," one security guard said.

Klouser laughed as he walked up to the gate.

"Hey mister, are you drunk or high? Then you shouldn't be out on the street," the other security guard said.

"You could say I'm high. High on a type of power that you normal humans would never understand," Klouser said right before he swung both of his blades and slashed a hole through the gate. The security guards ran back into the security room and shut the door. Klouser climbed through the hole in the gate, walked up to the door and kicked it open. One security guard was trying to phone for help while the other tried to attack him with his flashlight. Klouser slashed off a part of his hand and stabbed him in the throat, killing him instantly. He walked up behind the security guard who was trying to phone for help and knocked the phone out of his hand before he punched him in the face. He could have stabbed him and killed him, but instead, he beat him up. He punched him senseless until his face was a bloody mess. He took out one of those small strange-looking devices and stabbed it into the back of the security guard's neck, turning him into his new drone. After the device had taken control of the security guard's mind, he stood before him, waiting to follow his new master. The two climbed through the hole in the gate and continued walking down the street in search of Kathy and Trent.

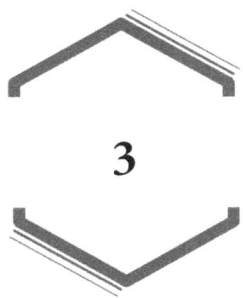

3

Kathy and Trent had been walking down the small town's main street in search of a place to hide, but they couldn't find one. All they found were small houses and shops. There weren't any empty houses or abandoned buildings they could hide in. They stopped when they reached the end of the main street.

"I think we should go to the next plane. Maybe it's somewhere deserted like the wastelands we've been to. Then we could hide there for a while," she said.

Unaware that Xanthy was dead, Trent said, "We can run and hide for a while, but we have to put our heads together and think of a way to defeat Klouser and Xanthy permanently. We have to end this. We can't spend the rest of our lives running from plane to plane and living in fear."

Kathy pulled him closer, hugged him and kissed him. The feeling of her warm embrace and intense passion of her kiss reminded him why he'd turned against Klouser and Xanthy. After a long kiss, he opened a portal door in the middle of the street and they moved on to the next plane.

A portal door opened on a field outside of a city. Many people from the city regularly came to this field to illegally dump their junk. There was everything from regular garbage to scrap metal to rusty pieces of trucks and cars as far as the eye could see. Kathy and Trent came out through the portal door and fell on top of a pile of scrap metal. As they tumbled down the pile, Kathy cut her leg on a sharp piece of metal plate. It was too dark for him to see she'd been injured but he heard her groan in pain.

"What is it? What's wrong?"

"My leg," she said through clenched teeth.

Trent made the palm of his hand glow and pointed it at her. The cut on her leg was deep and bleeding. He torn off his shirt and took her by the hand.

"This is gonna hurt. Squeeze my hand and think of anything to take your mind off of the pain."

He felt how hard she squeezed his hand when he pressed his torn shirt on the cut to try and stop the bleeding. She was squeezing his hand so hard that it was starting to hurt. Nevertheless, he kept a straight face as he said, "I know this hurts but I have to do this to minimize your blood loss while your wound heals."

In an attempt to take her mind off of the pain she was feeling, she tried to think of a way they could set a trap for their enemies. What Trent did next was totally unexpected. Still pressing his torn shirt on her cut, he put his other hand behind her head, leaned closer and kissed her. After a long passionate kiss, he began talking about anything and everything that popped into his mind. Asking her opinion about everything from how they could try different ways to fight Klouser and Xanthy, to what she would like to do on their first official date as a couple when they didn't have to fight or run for their lives anymore. Neither of them realized how long they were sitting and talking in the dark between the junk. She was so interested in everything they were talking about that she didn't notice that her cut had healed.

They stopped talking and looked at the faint glow of daylight as it slowly began lighting up the dark sky. Dawn. They both knew that this was a sign that they'd been on that plane for too long. They had to keep moving. They got up, dusted the dirt off their pants and kissed each other one more time. In the middle of their kiss, Kathy got such a big fright from the flash of blue light that she accidentally bit Trent's upper lip. A portal door opened on top of the pile of junk behind him. Klouser and his new drone came through the portal door. Kathy grabbed Trent by the hand and the two of them started to run between the piles of junk.

"Attack!" Klouser yelled as he began running after them. Following his master's command, the drone also ran after them. Kathy and Trent were running as fast as they could, hoping they could put enough distance between them and Klouser to buy them enough time to open a portal door and escape. Klouser and the drone were running side by side. He used his powers to send various items of junk flying through the air. A piece of twisted metal came flying past Kathy's head and a brick flew through the air, hit the pile of junk she was running past and shattered into tiny pieces. They changed direction and ran towards the street next to the field. When they reached the street, Klouser used his powers to send many items of junk flying off of one of the piles straight at them. An old broken microwave struck Kathy on the back of the head, and half of a pink surfboard struck Trent on his upper back, causing both of them to fall.

"They're coming! Get up!" Trent yelled. He scrambled to get up and as he moved towards her, he held his glowing hand out in front of him and began opening a portal door. Before he could reach her or open the portal door, the drone attacked him from behind. He struck him on the back of the head with his flashlight and began punching him when he turned around. Dazed by the blow to his head, Trent still fought back. Kathy got up and was about to attack the drone when Klouser attacked her and punched her. The first blow dazed her and the second one sent her stumbling backwards. Klouser pulled out both his blades, and yelled, "Xanthy is dead because of you! Both your powers will be mine!"

Trent fought the drone like a mad man. Punching him and kicking him, but every time he tried to pull out his blade, the drone attacked him again. Kathy pulled out her blade and attacked Klouser. She had to fight twice as hard and twice as fast because he fought with two blades like a pro. He slashed her across her abdominal area and kicked her. Seeing this, Trent wanted to help her and tried to attack Klouser. He let his guard down when he tried to run towards Klouser and the drone attacked him from behind. The drone struck him twice on the back of the head with his flashlight. He pulled out his blade and slashed the drone across the chest. Just as he wanted to stab his blade straight into the drone's chest, the drone struck him on the side of the head, knocked him down and jumped on top of him. Kathy slashed Klouser on his forearm, blocked his blades with hers, and tried to kick him in the groin but only managed to kick his knee.

"You fight dirty. I fight dirty too," he laughed.

Trent let out an angry groan as he pushed the drone off of him and got up. He wasn't going to let a drone stop him from helping Kathy to fight Klouser. The drone attacked him with his flashlight. Trent sliced of part of his forearm with one furious swing of his blade. He stabbed and slashed the drone across the chest numerous times before he finally unplugged him.

Kathy was being driven backwards by Klouser. He was fighting so fast with his two blades that she didn't get a chance to attack him. All she could do was dodge and block his blades. Trent tried to attack Klouser from behind. Aiming straight for the back of his neck, he was about to stab him when Klouser turned and blocked his blade. Judging by how he laughed at them, Klouser clearly thought that neither of them were a match for him. He took a few steps back as he fought Kathy with one blade, and Trent with the other. When he saw where the dead drone's body was, he slowly began moving backwards towards it. Kathy and Trent were fighting him side by side, looking for a way to injure him, to get him down on the ground so that they both could finish him off. Klouser kept glancing over his shoulder as he moved backwards until the drone's body was close enough. He blocked both their blades simultaneously, pushed them back, moved to the side and pointed his hand at the body. The drone's body flew through the air, struck Trent and sent him flying backwards through the air. Before Trent's body fell in the middle of the street, Klouser attacked Kathy. He slashed her and punched her before he opened a portal door right behind her. Dazed, Kathy could still hear Trent screaming, "Nooo!!!" right before Klouser grabbed her and forced her into the portal door. Trent pushed the body off of him and ran towards them, only to helplessly witness how Kathy and Klouser vanished into the portal door. By the time he reached the open portal door, it closed and vanished into the ground. He let out a scream filled with rage and despair. He couldn't believe Klouser had taken her. Tears dripped from his eyes as he opened a portal door and jumped into it. He didn't care how many planes he had to travel to and search through to find her. He wasn't going to rest until she was safe back in his arms. The big question burning in the back of his mind was: would she still be alive when he found her?

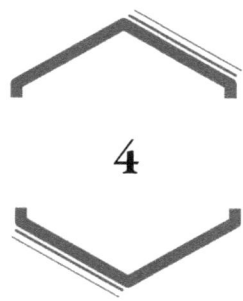

4

Kathy and Klouser came out through a portal door which opened behind an apartment building. Their bodies were slammed against a parked car, shattering two of its windows. Both began swinging their blades at each other before they even got up off the ground. Kathy rolled away from him, got up and attacked him. Sitting flat on his butt next to the car, he laughed as she tried to fight him and he effortlessly kept blocking her blade.

"Well, look who decided she was a big girl. Big enough to fight with the big boy," he laughed. "Put down your blade and join me. Become my new woman."

"Never!"

He used his powers to make the car's front door rip clean off of its hinges. It struck Kathy from the side and sent her body slamming into another car parked twenty feet away. Klouser got up and slowly walked towards her. Kathy used her powers to send the car door flying straight at him. He didn't bother to dodge it. He slashed it into pieces and sent the pieces flying over his head. She got up and ran towards him.

"You really think you can take me, little girl?" he laughed as he fought her.

"I'm not your little girl, and I'll never be your woman!"

She attacked him with all the fury in her. Her eyes were glowing. He tried to attack her but was forced to use both his blades just to keep blocking hers. He was so overconfident with all the powers he was feeling in his body that he laughed out loud like a mad man before he blocked her blade, hit her in the face with his elbow, pointed his glowing fist with the blade still in it over her shoulder, and opened a portal door behind her. She took a stab at his chest with her blade but he forced it down and it only slashed his hip before he rammed her with his shoulder and grabbed hold of her before they both vanished into the open portal door.

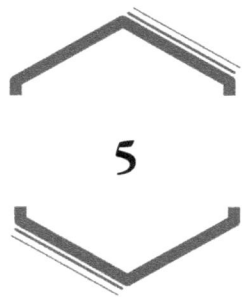

5

Trent came out through a portal door which opened in the middle of a dark country road. There were farms and ranches for many miles around him. He began calling out Kathy's name. Louder and louder until he was screaming her name like a lovesick lunatic.

He couldn't see much in the dark. That didn't stop him from running down the middle of the road, still screaming her name. He ran until he stepped in a small pothole in the road and fell. He got up, ignoring the pain from his sprained ankle, and continued running with a limp.

A short distance further, he stopped and screamed her name one more time. Not hearing anything, he wiped the tears from his face, opened a portal door and ran into it. He didn't care how many planes he had to go to to look for her. He wasn't going to stop until he'd found her. The big question was, was she still going to be alive when he did.

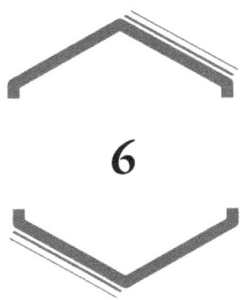

6

Kathy and Klouser came through a portal door which opened right in the middle of a graveyard. She fell on top of a grave and he fell next to it. She rolled off of the grave as he swung one of his blades and broke the grave's headstone. She got up jumped over the grave and tried to stab him. He kicked her in the stomach and sent her stumbling backwards. He got up and attacked her. As they fought, she was forced backwards. She bumped into a few headstones as she did everything she could just to block his attacks. Growing cockier by the second, he made the mistake of letting his guard down. Thinking that she would never be able to beat him, he held one of his blades up in the air above his head, as if to say to her: *'look, I can beat you with one hand.'*

She blocked his one-handed attacks until she did the unexpected. She kicked him in the stomach, blocked his blade with hers, punched him in the face, and slashed his hand, causing him to drop one of his blades. He tried to pick it up but couldn't. She attacked him and fought with such immense fury in her every move that she drove him backwards towards where they'd come out through the portal door. Moving backwards, he almost tripped twice. Not having two blades anymore meant that he had to fight twice as hard just not to give her a chance to stab him in the face, neck, or chest. He finally grew tired of being driven back and used his powers to make two of the headstones break in half as they flew out of the ground straight at her. She dodged two halves and shattered the other two with her blade. While she was doing this, Klouser opened another portal door right next to her. He attacked her, they locked blades, he grabbed hold of her and forced her into the portal door. Both of them vanished into the portal door, not know where they were going to end up next to continue their fight.

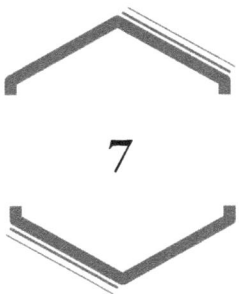

7

Trent came out through a portal door that opened on top of an office building. He looked around, ran to the edge of the roof and looked down at the city street down below. He screamed out Kathy's name and kept looking around down below. All he saw were four cars driving in the street down below. Other than that, he didn't see another soul down below. Something in his gut told him that Kathy wasn't on this plane. He looked back at the portal door and saw that it was starting to close. He ran to it and dove straight into it right before it closed.

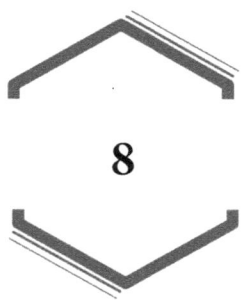

8

Kathy and Klouser came out through a portal door that opened on a small makeshift sports field close to more than fifty shacks at the foot of a hill outside of a small town. They hadn't just traveled to another plane of existence. They'd traveled to another continent. This was somewhere in Africa. The two continued to fight each other, oblivious to the fact that some of the locals had heard them fighting and had seen their glowing blue eyes and hands in the darkness. Some of the people ran away thinking that they were the angry ghosts of their ancestors or evil spirits. Kathy was fighting him with every ounce of planewalker power she had in her. As powerful and unstoppable as Klouser thought he was, he too was giving this blade battle his all. Beside using their blades, they both used their powers every time they saw something in the dark that they could use as a weapon. He used his powers to break the soccer goal apart and sent pieces of its wooden frame flying straight at her. She used her powers to send most of the pieces flying up into the air, sent five of the pieces straight back at him, and used her powers to make the goal's net wrap around him like a spider's web. He frantically fought to get out of the net. She attacked him and stabbed him twice in the stomach before he used his powers to send her body tumbling across the small field, all the way into the goal on the other side of the field. Klouser freed himself from the net and was still busy getting up off the ground when he heard her running towards him. He opened a portal door next to him. He blocked her blades with his and tried to grab hold of her to force her into the portal door, but he couldn't. She slashed his hand and punched him in the face. The portal door closed as they continued fighting each other.

9

Trent felt like he was losing his mind. To him, this felt like an endless night of failures. Every time he entered another plane and searched for Kathy, he felt how the hope of ever finding her alive was slowly slipping through his fingers. He'd lost count of how many planes he'd been to. Among others, he'd been to a number of alternate physical planes, the spiritual plane, and two wastelands. He'd even ended up in Hell, but then he immediately recognized the stench in the air and left again. As physically drained as he felt, as sore as his throat was from screaming her name so many times, as futile as it might have seemed to anyone else, he wasn't going to give up. He moved on to the next plane and continued his search for Kathy.

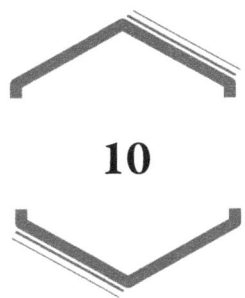

10

Kathy and Klouser were still fighting on the field. They'd been fighting each other so long that both of them felt drained of their energy. Some of the brave locals were hiding between the bushes next to the field, trying to see what was going on. Klouser had tried four times already to open a portal door and force her into it. He opened a portal door for the fifth time as they were fighting. He blocked her blade, grabbed hold of her and she began punching him. Every one of the blows to the face left him feeling like his head was spinning. He nevertheless still forced her into the open portal and they moved on to the next plane.

Trent was close to the entrance of a construction site outside of town. He called out Kathy's name as he ran between all the building materials. He reached a large open area that had been prepped for the factory that was going to be built there. He skidded to a stop, his feet almost slipping out from under him, when he saw the portal door opening. Kathy and Klouser came out through the portal door and continued fighting. With tears in his eyes, Trent screamed her name again as he ran towards them with his blade ready for battle.

"What?! You?!" was all Klouser said when Trent joined the fight. The three of them were so busy fighting that none of them noticed the faint blue glow moving around all over Kathy's body. What was happening to her? Was there something wrong with her powers?

Kathy kept fighting Klouser with Trent fighting by her side. She could feel strange sensations moving all over inside her body but she didn't take much notice of it. What she did notice however, was that she was growing stronger, gaining full control over her planewalker powers. Klouser stood his ground and fought them off with his blade. He could feel how all of this continuous fighting was starting to drain his strength. He slowly began moving backwards as he fought. Kathy and Trent thought they were finally gaining the upper hand in this fight, but Klouser was moving backwards for a reason. He was moving towards the piles of building materials and tools that were in the back of a dirty pickup behind him. He let out a rage-filled scream like a lunatic as he forced them back by attacking both of them with all his might before he turned around and ran towards the building materials. Kathy and Trent ran after him thinking that he was retreating and might open a portal door and try to escape. Klouser reached the pile of bricks next to the pickup and used his powers to send bricks flying at them. Kathy dodged three bricks before one struck her hip and another one struck her shoulder. Trent wasn't as lucky. His body was sent flying backwards when he was struck in the stomach by two bricks, struck on the chest by three, and struck in the groin by one. Dazed and in immense pain, his body struck the ground and skidded on the dirt. Fearing he might be badly hurt, Kathy made the mistake of glancing over her shoulder at Trent. When she looked back at Klouser, he was already using his powers to send all the tools in the back of the pickup flying at her. Instead of running out of harms way or dodging the flying tools, she used her powers to try and gain control of the tools. She sent most of them flying either to her sides or straight down into the ground. She sent two shovels flying straight back at him. Running towards him as he made the shovels break apart into tiny pieces before making them fly over his head, Kathy used her powers to make all the pickup's windows shatter. Every single shard struck Klouser either in the face, chest, stomach or arms. To him, the shards felt like bullets. As much as he wanted to scream out in pain, there wasn't time for him to do so. He had to fight through the pain and fight for his life as Kathy attacked him. He fought back in his weakened state.

Still dazed and winded, Trent got up and rushed to go help Kathy. He joined in the fight. Klouser's foolish pride made him think he still stood a chance at defeating both of them. He fought both of them simultaneously but couldn't manage to slash or stab either of them. He however was being stabbed in the chest and stomach, and slashed in the face. His pride finally crumbled to dust and he realized he was losing this battle, and that if he didn't make a run for it, it would be his last battle.

Klouser spat a mouthful of blood at them before he turned and ran from them. They ran after him as he was heading towards the entrance gate. He pointed his bloody glowing hand out in front of him and opened a portal door. Thinking that he was as good as gone, Klouser actually began laughing. As painful as it was for him to do so, he couldn't stop himself from laughing. Kathy slashed the back of his leg open. He didn't take his eyes off of the open portal door – which was only five feet in front of him – when he fell to the ground. He screamed at them to stop as Kathy slashed the back of his neck open. He tried to turn around only to feel how Trent's blade stabbed straight through his lower back, pinning him to the ground. Tears were dripping from his eyes as he began begging for his life. His cries for mercy turned into unintelligible sobs when he felt how Kathy's blade slashed his back open straight down the middle. Trent wanted to unplug him, but Kathy beat him to it. She mercilessly dug her fingers deep into the back of his neck and ripped out his spinal column. Klouser was finally unplugged. This moment felt unreal to Kathy and Trent. He pulled his blade out of Klouser's dead body and he was about to stab it a few more times to make sure the bastard was dead when he saw the blue glow moving in the dead body. He stepped back and witnessed how all of Klouser's powers left his body and were absorbed into Kathy's body. No words on earth could describe what she was feeling. All of

Klouser's powers, and the powers of all the planewalkers he'd killed, made Kathy's body hover four inches above the ground as they merged with her powers. The blue glow moving around inside her body started to fade as her feet touched the ground. Trent hugged her.

"You did it, Rosebud. We don't have to run anymore," he said.

Kathy was speechless. To her, Klouser had been the boogeyman that she'd feared. She couldn't believe the nightmare was over. She couldn't stop herself from crying as she kissed Trent. She wiped the tears from her eyes, looked at him, looked at the open portal door, and said, "Help me get him in there."

Trent helped her and they dragged Klouser's spineless body to the open portal door and pushed him into it.

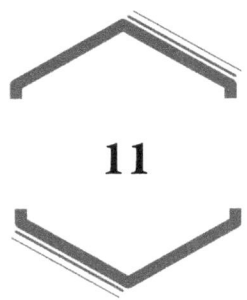

11

The portal door in the Transition Plane opened. Klouser's body hovered in the air. The five Guardians appeared and did what they always did. They made strange hissing noises as they moved around the body when they realized this wasn't just another planewalker. This was a dead one. They hissed louder as they moved around the body faster and faster until they faded into a blur. This torn Klouser's body apart. Each of his body parts were sent into a different portal door.

12

In Hell, Lucifer was sitting on his stone throne when Klouser's soul fell into the lake of fire. He gave a short yawn, as if to say that he was unimpressed by all the evil he sensed in his soul. The demons began torturing Klouser's soul as he began his eternity of much deserved punishment for his sins. Somewhere in the lake of fire, Xanthy's soul was also burning and being tortured. The two lovers and partners in crime were both in Hell, but as part of their punishment, they would never ever see each other again.

13

Kathy and Trent were still standing at the spot where she'd killed Klouser. Holding each other, happy and relieved that they didn't have to run for their lives and constantly look over their shoulders, both of them were wondering the same thing: *'Where do we go to from here?'*

On the one hand, she felt like finding a quiet place where the two of them could stay for a few days to get over the entire ordeal. But, in her mind, she kept seeing the faces of the other planewalkers they'd met.

Thinking that they had to celebrate their victory, Trent was about to suggest where they should go and what they could do to enjoy themselves together, but Kathy said, "We have to go somewhere. We've gotta go tell those other planewalkers that they don't have to hide anymore."

They kissed each other before she opened a portal door and they jumped into it.

Don't miss out!

Visit the website below and you can sign up to receive emails whenever Alec R. Zeelie publishes a new book. There's no charge and no obligation.

https://books2read.com/r/B-A-WNQE-NXPQB

BOOKS 2 READ

Connecting independent readers to independent writers.

Lightning Source UK Ltd.
Milton Keynes UK
UKHW040215310721
388036UK00015B/200